ZERO
AVeNuE

ALSO BY DIETRICH KALTEIS

Ride the Lightning

The Deadbeat Club

Triggerfish

House of Blazes

A CRIME NOVEL

ZERO
AVENUE

dietRich
Kal+Eis

ECW PRESS
TORONTO

Published by ECW Press
665 Gerrard Street East
Toronto, Ontario, Canada M4M 1Y2
416-694-3348 / info@ecwpress.com

Cover design and photograph: David Gee
Author photo: Andrea Kalteis

This is a work of fiction. Names, characters, places, and incidents either are the product of the author's imagination or are used fictitiously, and any resemblance to actual persons, living or dead, business establishments, events, or locales is entirely coincidental.

LIBRARY AND ARCHIVES CANADA CATALOGUING
IN PUBLICATION

Kalteis, Dietrich, author
Zero Avenue : a crime novel / Dietrich Kalteis.

ISSUED IN PRINT AND ELECTRONIC FORMATS.
ISBN 978-1-77041-365-8 (softcover)
ALSO ISSUED AS: 978-1-77305-079-9 (PDF),
978-1-77305-080-5 (EPUB)

I. TITLE.

PS8621.A474Z17 2017   C813'.6
C2017-902414-0   C2017-902993-2

The publication of Zero Avenue has been generously supported by the Canada Council for the Arts which last year invested $153 million to bring the arts to Canadians throughout the country, and by the Government of Canada through the Canada Book Fund. Nous remercions le Conseil des arts du Canada de son soutien. L'an dernier, le Conseil a investi 153 millions de dollars pour mettre de l'art dans la vie des Canadiennes et des Canadiens de tout le pays. Ce livre est financé en partie par le gouvernement du Canada. We also acknowledge the Ontario Arts Council (OAC), an agency of the Government of Ontario, which last year funded 1,709 individual artists and 1,078 organizations in 204 communities across Ontario, for a total of $52.1 million, and the contribution of the Government of Ontario through the Ontario Book Publishing Tax Credit and the Ontario Media Development Corporation.

Ontario
Ontario Media Development
Corporation

ONTARIO ARTS COUNCIL
CONSEIL DES ARTS DE L'ONTARIO
an Ontario government agency
un organisme du gouvernement de l'Ontario

Canada Council
for the Arts

Conseil des Arts
du Canada

Canadä

PRINTED AND BOUND IN CANADA   PRINTING: WEBCOM   5   4   3   2   1

TO ANDIE

... OCTOBER 1979
No Fun City

. . . KICKING IN THE STALL

FRANKIE DEL Rey's head was buzzing on the first toke, the locals calling it bhang, hash as good as any Kashmir or Nepalese. Could only get it from Marty Sayles's guys, and going out with him meant there was always plenty of it. Top it off, nobody fucked with her down here. The Eastside was a rough place, winos beaten for pocket change, old folks robbed of their pension cheques, one guy robbed of his dentures a couple days ago. Chicks carried knives or rocks in their bags after hours to keep from being violated. Punks traveled in groups to avoid a redneck shit-kicking. Rednecks coming down here figured anybody in tight black pants and leather was a fag. Couldn't tell the punks from the gays hanging out at the Quadra on Homer, the club where punk bands played every Wednesday. Punks and gays getting along. *Deep Throat* playing on the club's video screen day and night.

Marty Sayles ran the dope on the Eastside, and ran it with a fist. Muling for Marty kept her safe from anything but a drug bust. Frankie waiting for her music career to take off; meantime, this job beat any nine-to-five she could get, employers not hiring anybody looking punk. And to top it off, she was making double the pay for half the hours, compared to the guys in bands who worked graveyard at Royal Foods, getting drunk on something they concocted in the wee hours, calling it moose milk, joking about tossing their cigarette butts in the blueberry hopper and pissing in the cream corn vat, relieving the boredom of the long hours.

The ones who couldn't find work tried to jump on unemployment enjoyment, that or pogey. Most of them coming up with punk names like Stubby, Homo and Rude, names a case worker coming into a club wouldn't recognize. Arnie Binz, her bass player, wasn't bad at finding work, just had trouble hanging on to it.

First time they met, she caught a late-night ride with him, coming out of the Lotus, back when Arnie was driving a gypsy cab on a fake license. They got to talking on the ride home, Frankie saying she played guitar, Arnie telling her he played some bass, both loving punk. Arnie not charging her the fare.

A couple nights after they met, the cops pulled over Arnie's cab for a failed turn signal. The fake license landed him probation and a two-hundred-buck fine. Frankie ran into him again at a party the Sgt. Nick Penis Band was playing, the two of them talking about starting a band.

Her drummer, Joey Thunder, had lived on the street, back alleys, squatting in a condemned building on Gore Avenue for a while, living on beans and ketchup. Finally moved back with his folks after getting busted at the local thrift shop, switching his clothes for something off the rack, telling the beat cop it was cheaper than doing the laundry. Just walked in and changed, walked out with a new outfit. Third time busted for the same thing, so he did a little time and a lot of community service. Met Frankie and Arnie at a hall where Hammer was playing. The three of them sharing late-night joints and coffee, getting serious about it, deciding to call themselves Waves of Nausea.

Tough finding gigs and places to practice, but things had been picking up. Nearly had enough scratched together to lay down a seven-inch demo at Ocean Sound, place looking like a concrete bunker up in North Van. The plan was to get the EPs cut at Imperial or Saber Sound, get copies out to the fanzines and university radio stations, put some in hand with this guy Arnie met over at Perryscope, the city's biggest promoter. The plan was to land an agent and get themselves on a tour down the coast, playing places like the Mab in Frisco.

After the record was cut, she'd quit working for Marty. No more running his shit across the border, no more doing whatever it took.

Finding a parking spot along the south side of Hastings, she backed her Karmann Ghia in. Pushed in her lighter, put on another piece of bhang, put her mouth to the orange glow, drawing up the smoke. Holding it in, letting it out, that warm creeping starting in her feet, working its way up.

Yeah.

Parked behind some beat-to-hell Dodge van with Alberta plates, a sunset mural over rust wrapping around the side, stupid bumper sticker about not knocking when it's rocking. She could just make out the Smilin' Buddha's neon past it, up the block by Columbia. Ground zero for

Vancouver's punk scene. Any punk band would kill to play there.

Planned to drop in later, D.O.A. playing all week before they went back on tour, Joey Shithead doing alright since the Skulls split up, the new lineup kicking ass. Their song "The Prisoner" hitting Number One on the UBC's CITR. The guy getting hitched a few months back. The underground rags running headlines like Shithead Gets Married.

First stop tonight was Falco's Nest, just a couple doors past the van. The storefront of a seedy three-storey, the awning over the door claiming hot acts all the time. Cold beer sometimes.

Sucking in the last of the smoke, Frankie switched off the ignition, her car shuttering off. Yanking up the spongy parking brake, she pocketed the keys.

Just starting to spit rain. The street reflecting the traffic lights along Hastings. Somewhere a siren sounded from past Woodward's. Checking the backseat, she made sure she didn't leave anything of value. Unwritten law down here: don't lock your car doors unless you want a smashed window. Some junkie might think there was something worth hiding. Worst thing that might happen, one of the homeless could curl up on your backseat, leave a stain and a funky smell.

Flipping up her denim collar, she popped out the portable Craig deck and stepped into the street. A taxi honking. Frankie throwing the cabbie the finger. Locking the deck in the trunk with her Flying V, she walked past the mural van, a Doberman hurling itself against the passenger window, snarling and baring its teeth. The whole van rocking. Sent

4

Frankie's heart into her throat. Giving the dog the finger, she told it to fuck off.

Marty Sayles's Toronado was parked out front, Zeke Chamas watching her from behind the wheel, grinning at her. Zeke back to playing chauffeur.

Marty had called her after taking care of some business at Lubik's, wanting to get together for a late dinner, asked if she liked Italian, said he booked them a table. This place Paesano's along Broadway was the best, the old woman who ran the kitchen made the pasta from scratch. Frankie guessed the third date with Marty meant he'd be asking her up to his place in the Properties for a nightcap, the boss looking to round the bases, not likely to settle with another peck on the lips.

Frankie had been in the front seat the night of Marty's DUI. Out to dinner and a show at the Rio, Marty wanting to see *Alien*. Both of them doing lines of coke, taking in a couple of clubs after, Marty ordering up champagne, showing his dance moves and making like he was hip. Driving her home after, he was going on about the chest-buster scene, then talking about the preview of *10*, Bo Derek running on the beach. Eyes wandering from the road, hand wandering to her thigh. Making his move when the cop's cherry flashed in the rearview. Taking his hand back, Marty pulled to the curb and rolled down his window, ended up wagging a twenty at the cop. The wrong cop. Marty was told to step out and assume the position, his hands sprawled on the Toronado's roof, the cop asking if he'd been drinking.

Frankie guessed Marty was here tonight collecting the back rent from Johnny Falco, one of a string of slums he

5

owned. Liked handling the cash himself. Zeke Chamas driving him around town, backing him up.

Arm hanging out the window now, Zeke watched her walk up from behind, fingers tapping the steering wheel. The tinny AM playing "Afternoon Delight."

Sky rockets in flight.

She leaned down and gave him a wave through the passenger window. Zeke flicking a salute, looking bored.

Frankie needed to stretch things out with Marty without losing the job running his dope. The plan was to break it off as soon as she had all the cash together. Cut the record and get out of town.

. . . FALCO'S NEST

SHE WALKED in, Falco's Nest open to the indie music scene. Johnny Falco being the second club owner with the balls to do it. Most venues around town treated punk like taboo: pogo dancing leading to underaged drinking, leading to drunken fist fights, leading to police raids and shutdowns.

Johnny moved here from back east, got to know the punk scene in Toronto, told her about living in the Lawrence Hotel, rooms like two bucks and change a night, a Sabbath cover band called Never Say Die stayed down the hall, the band living on potatoes and soup packets. Getting to know them while bowling with empty ketchup and beer bottles in the hall, driving the landlord crazy.

She loved hearing Johnny tell about the Toronto scene: the Viletones, the Demics. Bands like the Diodes, Cardboard Brains and Teenage Head out of Hamilton, venues like Larry's Hideaway on Carlton. Johnny saying he wished he'd been on the coast to catch the Furies before they split up, loved their sound, getting out here a couple years too late.

Photos were tacked up behind the bar: him standing arm in arm with Frankie Venom, another one of him and Daniel

Rey, producer for the Ramones, one with Carole Pope out front of the Concert Hall.

Lachman over at the Buddha was first to do it in Vancouver, bringing the sound to town. The Young Canadians, still called the K-Tels back then, put on a hell of a show, followed by the Subhumans. The Buddha had been packed ever since, Lachman still trying to live down the night he kicked out Hendrix, back in the club's R&B days a decade earlier, Lachman telling anybody who'd listen the guy just played too loud.

Falco's Nest had been catching the Buddha's overflow since opening its doors eight months back. Johnny usually short on cash, but long on ideas, showcasing new talent, giving bands a chance to jump off the hamster wheel of shit gigs available to them. The local papers called both clubs a spawning ground for a new terrorism on the sensibilities, but Vancouver's punk scene didn't read the dailies — fans flocking from as far as Mission, giving the "No Fun City" image a good shake.

Not sure who Johnny had booked in tonight, she walked by the posters plastered across the storefront window. Hoping to duck Marty till later, she'd come to hear some music, have a beer with Johnny then drop in at the Buddha, catch some of D.O.A.'s second set. The guys sometimes letting her sit in. Her Flying V locked in the trunk, just in case.

She stepped into the warmth and the smoke. The biker blocking the door was Stain, big as a bear, tattooed arms hanging from under the Hellrazors MC vest. Fingerless gloves and fingers thick as brats. Never charged her the cover. Everybody else paid two bucks to get in, half a buck less than the Buddha. The way it went at Falco's, if Stain didn't like your looks, it cost you three bucks to get back out. The two bucks went to Johnny, the three going to Stain.

She gave Stain a hug, kissing his cheek, then scanned the room. Black walls, exposed ceiling, graffiti and more band posters plastered on every wall. Johnny's idea of decorating. The floods shone on four skinny guys setting up on the crappy stage of nailed crates. Lead, rhythm, bass and a guy keeping the beat.

"Marty here?"

Stain shrugged like he hadn't noticed, no love lost between him and anybody else dealing dope in here. Johnny's rule: Stain broke up the fights, warned him when the cops or anybody looking like an inspector walked in the door, but he didn't make trouble with Marty Sayles, the drug-dealing landlord. For that, Stain got free beer and nine bucks an hour, triple the minimum wage.

A decent mid-week crowd tonight. A couple of guys from the Braineaters, Zippy Pinhead over talking with Monk, another Hellrazor. Frankie thinking Zippy was one of the hottest drummers around, right up there with Robert Bruce, not something she'd admit to her own drummer, Joey Thunder.

Underage kids in torn denim and leather milled around the stage, sucking on beer bottles, set to pogo. An old rummy stood propped against the far wall by the co-ed can, getting out of the cold long enough to stop the shakes, Stain giving the guy a pass, sometimes slipping him a couple of bucks, showing he had a heart. Once the old guy warmed up, he'd move on.

"Hey ya." Folding her hands on the bar, Frankie smiled at Johnny Falco, the Carling O'Keefe neon flickering behind him like it might go out.

"Hey yourself." Smiling back, he reached in the cooler, drew out a dripping stubbie, knowing her brand. Sliding the ov across.

"Who we got tonight?" Frankie nodded at the stage.

"Middle Finger — drove in from Calgary, their van conked out front, out of gas."

The one with the bumper sticker and freaky dog. Frankie saying, "They any good?"

"Real good, yeah. Here the rest of the week."

She slapped a buck on the bar, Johnny sliding it back. Bands, bikers and friends drank for free. Johnny's rule.

Pocketing the buck, she thanked him and tipped the bottle up, her eyes on his.

Johnny asking how she was doing.

"Getting by, you know. Working on some new tunes." Telling him the Waves were putting some original stuff down, tight on a half dozen covers now. Johnny asking what she was doing for rehearsal space. Frankie telling him about the barn out on Zero Avenue, Marty Sayles owning it like he owned this three-storey shithole, letting the Waves practice out in the boonies. One of the perks for running his dope and going out with the guy.

Her bass player, Arnie Binz, edged his way through the crowd, coming from the back room with a couple cases of beer, Arnie working here three nights a week. His flop up on the top floor, with a shared bathroom at the end of the hall. Worked here since getting canned from the 7-Eleven night shift — caught stuffing comics into his guitar case — the job he landed after he got busted driving the gypsy cab.

Arnie set the cases on the bar, gave her a smile. Told Johnny he ought to switch to cans, easier to carry. Johnny said he'd think about it, sending him back for more.

Middle Finger kicked it off. Johnny passed beers to hands reaching across the bar, stuffing dollar bills into his old-style National register, brass with a crank on the side. The dollar and cents flags popped up every time he hit the lever, opening the drawer. Frankie bopped her head, the guitar player slaying some licks, shrieking into the mic about confused teens. The crowd was getting into it, pogoing, screaming and drinking.

Three tunes in, she felt the need to pee; Frankie sipped her way to the co-ed can, knowing better than leaving a beer unattended.

Slapping Monk's outstretched hand, she made her way across the floor, said hey to Pinhead, weaving past jumping bodies, shoving open the door, the filthiest can this side of CBGB. Fifty bands had passed through Falco's Nest since Johnny lifted a toilet brush. Anytime somebody complained, he'd say, "That's punk for ya."

Johnny took the bottles from the case, putting them in the big cooler. Realized he forgot to tell her Marty Sayles had been in, not sure if he'd gone, the guy pissed off on account of the back rent. Johnny telling him he'd have it in a day or so, same thing he always told him.

●

Sucking a breath, Frankie stepped in. *Freaky loo* sprayed in hot pink over the mirror, paint that had dripped down the wall and over the glass. *Get Modern or Get Fucked* scrawled across the ceiling.

A lone bulb hung from the center of the room, a dead fluorescent tube horizontal over the sink, two toilets, only one with an enclosed stall, a urinal and a plugged-up sink, soapy brown scum floating in it. Toilet paper unfurled like crime scene tape across the floor. Graffiti all over — the voice of the people.

Frankie's eyes adjusted to the dim, a guy in a sport jacket stood pressed against the wall, his head tipped back, Adam's apple bobbing, the guy groaning over the pounding music. A girl on her knees, giving him the business. Frankie thinking *ewww*, people having sex in this place, worse than joining the mile-high club.

Halfway through saying "Get a room," Frankie recognized him, turning it into "Jesus, Marty?"

Hearing his name, Marty Sayles focused his eyes, his hands on the girl's head like he was holding himself steady. The blonde craned her neck, her lipstick smeared, eyes of someone on opioids.

There it was, her way out. Frankie put her free hand on her hip, acting pissed, saying, "What happened to having dinner?"

Marty pushed the head away, fumbling at his pants, saying that was later.

"How about take a fucking number." The blonde made the mistake of getting up, putting her hands on her own hips.

Frankie threw the bottle and missed. An explosion

of beer and glass against the tiles. Setting the blonde off, shrieking and rushing at Frankie, her fingers up like claws.

Growing up on the Eastside, Frankie knew how to scrap, put some hip into it and threw a fist. Caught the blonde on the beak, but didn't stop her. The claws coming again. Hit her again and snatched a fistful of blonde, twisting her head around. Getting her shoe up, Frankie sent her sprawling to the wet floor, the blonde smacking her head on the scummy toilet, the girl sagging down, legs flopping on the floor.

Stuffing his shirt in his pants, dress shoes slipping on beer suds, Marty caught himself against the wall, yelling, "What the fuck, Frankie!" High on coke and the poppers he took off some pusher Zeke beat up, Marty pulled himself together, wondering where the fuck was Zeke. The blonde was useless to him now, lying flopped across the toilet, her hair in the bowl, streaks of blood showing like dark roots. "Look what the fuck you did."

"You know what, Marty, pretty much lost my appetite," she said. "And this you and me thing, it ain't working out." Stepping to the toilet, Frankie raised her Converse and pressed the lever, flushing, the blonde hair swirling, getting sucked down the bowl.

Turning for the door, she said, "She comes around, tell her to get her head examined while they're stitching it up."

"What you and me thing?" Marty called as she walked out the door. Too high for this. Using the toe of his dress shoe, Marty eased the blonde's head from the toilet to the wet floor. Still putting together what just happened, he tried to recall the girl's name. Sally or something. Wondering again where the fuck Zeke was.

The band was kicking it, covering one by the Hot Nasties, the bass player screaming and spitting into the mic about Barney Rubble being his double.

The rest of the band backing the vocals with their *yabba dabba do*s.

The crowd loving it.

Shaken, but relieved the thing with Marty was over, Frankie was thinking in *Georgia Straight* headlines: Drug Kingpin Fellated in Filthiest Can This Side of CBGB. Angling past the people crowding the bar, she caught Johnny's eye.

"Something wrong, no TP?" Snapping off beer caps, Johnny caught her mood, practically shouting to be heard.

"Your toilets, Johnny . . ." Frankie leaned across the bar, putting a hand on his, saying, "enough to make Mr. Clean hurl." She walked for the door.

Yabba dabba fucking do.

A group of boppers pushed their way in, their arms around Jughead, drummer for the Modernettes, holding up his drunken ass. Stain collecting the cover, telling Jug he better learn to hold his fucking liquor.

Jug saying the lickers were doing just fine, reaching in a pocket, tossing up a bunch of bills, enough for everybody's cover, saying, "Hey ya, Frankie."

●

STEPPING INTO the rain, she went around the lineup out front, like a party in the street, didn't matter it was raining. Miss Lovely, the Eastside's preaching ex-hooker stood talking to some young chick with braces on her teeth. Sixty years old and wobbling on her heels, Miss Lovely wore fishnets that bunched at her ankles. Reaching in a pocket, Frankie pressed the buck she didn't pay Johnny for the beer into the old woman's hand, Lovely thanking her.

From behind the wheel of the Toronado, Zeke Chamas watched Frankie. She looked pissed, walking and yelling at some geezer who was yanking open her car door. The geezer looked up from the Ghia, starting toward her past the mural van. The Doberman jumped against the passenger window, teeth smacking the glass, freaking out Frankie and the geezer, Frankie yelling at it, inches from the glass. Zeke watching and laughing.

The crowd outside Johnny's egged her on, hoping for a fight: punk chick versus attack dog.

Coming out the door, Stain told everybody to shut the fuck up. Last thing Falco's needed was the cops pulling up again — the boys in blue dying to close this place down, the Main Street station only about a block away. Stain told the geezer to keep moving, then threw a look Zeke's way, the Toronado at the curb, the two of them eyeing each other, nothing friendly about it.

. . . GIMME DANGER

ONE THING for sure, Marty Sayles wasn't hanging around, didn't matter he owned the place. A guy known to police. A couple days and he'd get his license back. Leaving the girl, Sally, lying on Falco's tiles, Marty went past the bar, smacking down his fist, telling Johnny he better clean up in there, saying again he wanted that overdue rent. Didn't give a shit how he got it. And walked out.

Shoving his way to the street, Marty walked to his car, the swagger of a guy who owned this place and three more rat traps just like it. Marty betting the blocks between the Carnegie Library and Victory Square were ripe to gentrify, sitting this close to downtown. The writing was on the wall, with places like the Pacific Centre popping up. People starting to look at Vancouver as more than an outpost, migrating from back east, Asians moving in.

Zeke sat behind the wheel, stupid pop music playing on the radio — Toni Tennille singing about doing it to her one more time. Rain dripping on his head, Marty got set to drop a ton of shit on Zeke Chamas, the guy supposed to be watching his back. He'd been thinking he needed to insulate himself from the business side of things, and Zeke Chamas was just the guy to put in charge. Get him to make his collections and see that packages got dropped off on time. Liked the way the guy handled himself at Lubik's this morning. The two of them had walked in, the cafe packed with kids ordering the ninety-nine-cent breakfast before the place stopped serving it at eleven thirty. Zeke Chamas slipped the blackjack up his sleeve, cupping his hand to keep it there. One of the guys they came to see — name of Digger — was sitting at a table at the back, a decade older than anybody else in the place, glancing up as Marty and Zeke walked up.

"You know me?" Marty Sayles had said to the guy. Word on the street was two dealers had drifted in from Port Moody, selling dime bags to the eighth-graders skipping from Strathcona Elementary. Been doing it about a week now.

Lifting an eyebrow, Digger said, "You boys from the school, huh?"

Zeke saying, "Yeah, school of hard knocks."

Digger grinning at him.

The waitress swung by and set a plate of eggs and toast in front of Digger, asking Marty if they needed menus.

"Won't be staying," Marty told her, waiting till she left, then looked back at Digger.

"Mind passing the ketchup?" Digger pointed to the next table.

Looking, Marty said to Zeke, "Fella wants his ketchup."

Reaching past the kids at the next table, Zeke asked if they minded, taking the bottle and setting it by the guy's plate.

"Thanks. Now, you gonna tell me what's on your mind, fellas, before my eggs go cold?" Digger uncapped the bottle, turned it upside down and tapped the bottom, blobbing some on his plate, then picking up his fork.

Marty looked to Zeke, saying, "Don't want his eggs going cold."

Zeke let the blackjack slip down his sleeve, catching the leather strap, swinging it up and cuffing Digger on the chin. Nearly knocked him from his chair. Did it so fast, nobody in the place noticed.

Catching an arm, Zeke lifted Digger up, strong for his size. Blood leaking from between Digger's teeth looked like the ketchup off his plate. Zeke steered him for the back door. Marty snagged the gym bag off the extra chair, the waitress coming back with the coffee pot, seeing the untouched plate, Zeke helping the customer out the back, the girl asking Marty if he was alright.

"Not so sure these eggs are fresh, hon," Marty said, taking out his wallet, laying down a couple of bucks, saying they ought to be checking for that kind of thing, then he followed Zeke out the back door. The girl looked puzzled, lifted the plate, gave it a sniff. Pocketing the bills, she went to the next table, offering refills. Teens all lost in chatter, nobody paying attention.

Out back, Zeke went to work with the blackjack, enjoyed hitting the guy. One to the back of the head, then a blow to the back of a knee, sending Digger stumbling around.

Pulling his switchblade, Digger flicked it open, steadying himself on the wall, putting his back to the bricks. Timing it, he lunged with the knife.

Feinting left, ducking the blade, Zeke knocked it away. Then he kept swinging, good with the club, showing Marty what he could do, cracking a few ribs, ringing Digger's bell a couple more times, putting him down, giving him a few short chops for good measure.

Marty saying that was enough.

Reaching inside the guy's jacket, Zeke took out his wallet, helping himself to a couple hundred in cash, then tossed the wallet down.

Marty unzipped the gym bag: dime bags of pot, poppers and bennies in pill containers. Standing over Digger, he said, "You come back, my friend here'll make it permanent, understand me?" Taking the grunt as a yes, Marty took the bag and walked from the alley, saying, "Enjoy your eggs."

Zeke dropped the blackjack back in his pocket, following behind Marty, feeling better about things after having to drive Marty around town in his Toronado the past few months.

Now Marty got back in the car, figuring he'd give Zeke some shit about watching his back, sharpen him up, then remind him he was in line to run things once Marty got his license back. Marty wanting to step back from the day-to-day business, thinking if the cops ever cracked down, Zeke Chamas would be his insulation, the guy who'd take the fall.

. . . THE BACK RENT

HANDING MONK the keys to his Scout, Johnny took Sally's legs, torn pantyhose and spiky red pumps, helped get the blonde out the back way. Monk taking her weight and loading her onto the passenger seat, the blonde in need of some stitches, blood mixing with the dye job. Johnny felt bad, but didn't need the cops busting in and rousting everybody for ID, closing him down for the night — again. The cops itching to make it permanent.

Monk asked what went down in the can, walking around the two Harleys parked next to Johnny's ride.

Johnny said he wasn't sure; guessing by the way Frankie walked out, she'd got in a fight. He hoped she was done with Marty Sayles. There had been a spark between her and Johnny since he first caught the Waves at 343 Railway, a hangout for artists, over by the Japanese Hall. Frankie and the band walking in with a case of beer that time, her guitar case over her shoulder. The artists reached for the beer, and the band got to play. Getting some exposure, but no pay. Frankie cranked away on that Flying V. Johnny seeing the girl had something, asking her to grab a coffee after, the two of them talking into the night.

Didn't need Hilly Kristal to tell him this girl had talent, the real deal. Johnny thinking about her now, not much of it having to do with playing guitar. Johnny saying to Monk that guy Marty was a jerk.

"Yeah, but not one you fuck with. Heard him and Zeke caught some pusher coming in from Port Moody today. Marty and Zeke dragged him out back of Lubik's, spoiling his ninety-nine-cent breakfast." Monk reached the driver's door handle, saying, "You still owe him rent?"

"Three months counting this one," Johnny said. In spite of the crowds, Falco's Nest was barely scraping by.

"You need some cash . . ." Monk said. "Might have a way."

"Don't want to borrow any more." Johnny looking at the girl bleeding on his seat.

"Not that. Word is Marty's growing his own. His guys patching weed in cornfields. Got over a dozen farms, maybe more, between here and Abbotsford. The way I hear it, his guys take out a couple rows of corn, stick in their own crop. The corn grows up around it and hides it."

"Farmers let him do it?"

"Don't think he's asking."

Arnie Binz stepped from the back door into the alley, in the shadows, a bag of trash in his hand. The unconscious girl in Johnny's Scout. Monk telling Johnny about this farm down by the border, Marty Sayles owning the place through some shell company, using the barn for curing, whatever else he had going. A couple of his boys keeping watch, an armed presence to the locals. Monk saying, "Letting the rubes know what happens if somebody calls the cops, you know, messes in his business."

"How about we do this later?" Johnny said, looking in at the blonde.

Monk not in a hurry, saying, "You hit a field and your back rent's history." He thumped a fist on the roof, seeing Arnie in the shadows, saying to Johnny, "You interested, we'll talk later."

"Don't think so, but thanks." Johnny anxious, looking at the blonde.

"Yeah, well, you change your mind, I can line you up with this guy I know, buy all you can grab. For two bills, I draw you the map." Monk pulled open the door. "Be like money in the bank." He started to get in, hesitated, saying, "Do it myself, but word come down from on high, 'Hellrazors don't mess in Marty Sayles's business. Don't fuck with him, he don't fuck with us.'" Getting in, he turned the key, Monk backing Johnny's orange Scout, leaving him to think about it.

"Could get us a better stage," Arnie Binz said, stepping from under the bulb by the back door, putting the lid on the can, watching Monk drive off.

Us.

"Supposed to be watching the bar," Johnny said, turning for the back door.

"Taking my break, plus Stain's got an eye on it."

"Since when you get breaks?" Johnny walked to the door, looking at him, this guy going union.

"Got to drain the vein now and again, you know?"

"Out here?"

"Yeah, you seen your toilets, man?" Arnie smiling.

"Come out and listen in on men talking."

Arnie shrugged, saying, "How about you and me?"

"You and me what?"

"I know the field, one Monk's talking about, fact I'm the one told him about it. Surprised he's cutting me out. But, you and me, the two of us, go and do a little reaping. Save you the two bills. We just split what we grab."

Johnny pulled open the door, Middle Finger ending their set. "Thought you had to leak," he said. Then told Arnie to clean the blood off his car seat when Monk got back, letting the door shut, leaving Arnie in the alley.

. . . KILLER WEED

STILL THINKING about it when he closed up. Some quick cash could mean changing out the plywood and crates he'd pulled from the alley, the makeshift stage starting to rot. Could use a better PA, too. The used JBLs from the Stone Age. That and catching up on the rent, getting Marty Sayles off his back. Marty saying he didn't give a shit how Johnny got the money, long as he got it.

Down to eighty bucks in the till from the beer sales after he paid Middle Finger for the night, guys from the other side of the Rockies. The singer was a guy named Art, slammed his head into Johnny's plaster during the encore. Striking a joist left Art dazed and bleeding, the crowd loving it, shouting for more, like it was part of the act. Second head in need of stitches tonight.

The band loaded up their van, Johnny guessing they were sleeping in there with the dog. He handed Art a beer, Art holding ice wrapped in a T-shirt to his skull, Johnny telling him about the Plaza, a place where the band could crash, lots of room and a fireplace mantle made from an old Pontiac grille. Thanking him, Art said they were running on fumes, in need of some gas before they drove anywhere. Johnny telling him about an all-night Esso a few blocks along Hastings. Then they talked about the tour, four of them sharing motel rooms when they got paid, getting spit at in some dive in a place called Sioux Lookout. Refused service at a roadside joint in Portage la Someplace. Yokels at some club called Ruby's in Moose Jaw ran them off, couldn't get enough of "Bud the Spud." The locals not ready for anything like punk.

One more night here and the band was hauling ass down the coast: opening for the Lewd in Seattle, lined up a community hall gig in Tacoma, on to Portland for two nights with the Wipers, then a night with the Angry Samoans in L.A., turning the van around after some fun in Tijuana. Back here in a month for a gig booked at PUMPS. The kind of tour Frankie del Rey had talked about, the girl dying to take Waves of Nausea on the road.

Monk and Stain had cleared everyone out, Art heading to the van, in need of some sleep, Arnie working the push broom. Stain set the gate on the bar, just shy of a hundred bucks, saying, "Weekend'll be better." Knowing it wouldn't be, tapping his fist on the stack.

"Yeah." Johnny offered Monk a twenty for taking the chick to emergency, Monk waving it off, sold enough hash on the night, said he didn't need it. Stain making enough charging the drunks three bucks to get out. Handing Johnny some tinfoil with a couple lines, Stain saying he looked like he could use it.

"About that map . . ." Johnny said to Monk, counting off

a few more bills, setting them down, half of what the big man wanted. "Said you got a buyer, huh?"

Looking at the shortfall, Monk sighed, said yeah, then took it. Johnny popped three beers, sliding two across the bar, sitting on the stool, realizing it was the first time he'd sat all night. Arnie worked the broom, shaking his head to a tune he was humming, making like he wasn't listening in. Johnny telling him to go sweep over by the stage.

Finding a pen next to the register, Johnny handed it to Monk, Monk marking up a napkin, saying, "Sayles got fields all over." This being the one he knew about for sure, not saying how he found out. Saying the pot was planted in rows between the corn, drawing in the T intersection, Zero Avenue and the townline. "Should be a hundred plants or so. Marty's guys are doing the same thing in fields all the way out to Chilliwack."

Johnny whistled, thinking about it, watching Monk finish the map.

"Do it the one time only. These assholes find out they been ripped off, going to come looking, understand?"

Johnny nodded.

Tipping back his beer, Monk wrote a phone number in the corner, wrote the name Murphy under it, told him he'd let him know Johnny would call, slid the map across the bar.

"When?"

Monk shrugged, saying, "They got to harvest ahead of the frost, right? So I wouldn't wait."

"These guys armed?"

"What do you think?"

"And I guess they won't be shooting rock salt," Johnny said.

"Somebody shoots, you shoot back."

Simple.

"Important you don't get seen, right? Maybe get a different ride," Monk said. "That thing of yours sticks out."

Johnny guessed these two had been warned off by their prez to leave Marty Sayles alone on account of what happened at their clubhouse in White Rock. He knew better than to ask if it was true: half the bikers getting run off by a mob of pissed-off dads. Kicking in the door, wielding clubs and bats. The bikers drunk and caught off guard. The dads rushed in swinging, beating drunken bikers senseless, looking for teenaged daughters that weren't there. Bikers and their old ladies pouring from the doors, jumping out windows. Those who could, ran into the night. A blow to the brotherhood, half of them quitting right then, leaving town or patching over.

Shoving the hundred bucks in a pocket, Monk headed for the exit, saying if Johnny scored big, he expected the other hundred, saying this wasn't a charity, then asking who he had playing the weekend.

Johnny saying the Dishrags, Monk saying those underage chicks could play, then the two of them went out the back door.

The bikes fired up in the alley and pulled away, Arnie taking out the last of the trash, locking up the back.

"Waves of Nausea got a gig this weekend?" Johnny said to Arnie, sorry he didn't get a chance to ask Frankie.

Arnie shook his head. "Practicing at the barn," Arnie

said, a quick glance at the map on the bar, recognizing the T intersection, the farm out on Zero Avenue. Pot growing in the corn out back of where they rehearsed. Could have told Johnny that much for free, same way he had told it to Monk, the guy who just sold Johnny the map. Arnie wishing he'd kept it to himself.

Folding it away, Johnny looked at the time, thinking he'd wait till tomorrow, after he scored a few sacks of weed, call Frankie up, ask her to catch the Dead Kennedys at the Legion Hall, the gig a couple of weeks off, give him a reason to call her. After he sold the weed to Monk's guy, he'd have some walking-around money.

Saying goodnight, Arnie went out the front, locking up. The door next to the club led up the stairs to his room.

Wiping the bar top, Johnny wondered where he could get his hands on a van or truck. Emptying the coke from the foil, he tapped it with a credit card and made two lines, took a deuce from the till and rolled it up. Under the neon beer light, he did one line, tipped his head back, let it ride, then did the other. Turning on the crap TV over the bar, he adjusted the aerials, the late news wrapping up, something about the Ayatollah, angry crowd shots in the Middle East, people burning flags, then an interview with Maggie Thatcher talking economic policy. Johnny turned the volume down, watching her mouth move, got to thinking about Frankie, pictured her handling Marty in the can, knocking out the blonde. Would have paid to see it.

Reaching the cc from under the bar, he sat on the stool, looked at the bottle and thought why not? Splashed some in a glass and stared at the map, drinking and pouring shots, the sports wrap-up on the tube showing highlights from the Holmes-Shavers match from last week, eleventh-round TKO. Johnny pouring till he was too drunk to drive home.

Then it came to him. He looked out the front window, went and grabbed an armload of beer bottles and took them out to Middle Finger's van three doors up. He tapped the door with his foot, the Doberman freaking out, snarling at the window, showing teeth.

Rolling down the window, Art said, "What the fuck, man?" Seeing the beer, he told the dog to shut up.

Johnny asked if the band wanted to crash inside, was lots more room in his club, plus there was a can. When they were all inside, he asked if he could borrow the van in the morning, said he'd put in a tank of gas.

. . . GO FUCK YOURSELF, MARTY

"WHAT FUCKING time is it?" Marty said, his voice sounding groggy over the phone.

Frankie looked at the clock on the stove, told him, "Nearly one."

"Ah . . . a real pisser, you know that?"

"Surprised you can sleep," Frankie said, hearing Marty cover the mouthpiece, sure she heard a female voice in the background. Betting it was the same blonde, Marty offering comfort.

"What you saw, look . . . that was just business. Woman owed me from last week. Know I got to collect when people owe me."

"Worked it out in trade, huh?"

"Meant nothing. Was a little drunk, you know how I get."

"But of all places . . . Jesus, Marty."

"Was high, top of that, I took a couple poppers, mixed with the booze . . . Why am I explaining to you?" More muffled voice. Frankie glad it was over, but wanting to know she still had the job.

"Thing you want to remember . . ." Marty said. The

sound of his hand covering the phone, Marty telling some-body to shut up.

"What, me working for you?" Frankie said.

"Pretty sweet deal, you ask me."

"What's not working is the you and me thing."

"What thing? We go out a couple times, you call it a thing?"

"Just to be clear."

"Clear, you want clear?" Marty sounding pissed, saying, "Ought to think who's five years past L.A."

"What's that even mean?"

"Means you're not getting younger, Frankie. And in the music biz . . ."

"The hell you know about it? Tell you what, Marty . . ." The anger rising, this guy with the fucking receding hairline going gray, talking about not getting younger. "Next bimbo gets off her knees, have her spit, get her to run your shit. See how it works out." Smacking down the receiver, the cord all looped around. Frankie flung the phone off the counter. Bouncing off the fridge, giving her dial tone. Kicked her bare foot at it. Felt the pain shoot up her leg.

Five years past L.A.

Then thinking, shit, what did she just do.

•

"MARTY AGAIN?" Rita Myles walked into the kitchen, Lily of France panties and a tank top. Rita with the nice curves. Didn't let Frankie call her Auntie, the woman defying her own age. Rita looked at the clock on the stove, bending for the phone, picking it up, untangling the cord and setting it back on the counter. Running a hand through her usually coiffed hair, she put the receiver to her ear, checking it was still working, setting it back in the cradle. Reached the Bounty dispenser, tearing off a sheet and passing it.

"Sorry I woke you," Frankie said, blowing her nose. "The guy's such an asshole."

"Language."

"Sorry."

Pulling the door of the old Kelvinator, Rita reached a tub of Danone, one with the fruit on the bottom, strawberry, setting it next to the phone. Getting bowls and spoons, saying, "Want to tell me?" Peeling the lid off the tub, Rita ladled yogurt into the bowls. Slid one across the counter.

Dipping her spoon, Frankie took a taste, saying it wasn't bad, telling Rita she caught Marty cheating, didn't mention the blonde on her knees, or where she caught him. "Asshole says I'm five years past L.A., you believe that?"

"Language."

"Sorry." Frankie sighed, left the yogurt and went to the adjoining living room, lifting her Flying V from its stand, sitting on the sofa arm, the guitar across her lap. Strumming it unplugged, she turned the peg, tuning the A.

Rita had been there that day at the pawn shop across from the Laundry Lounge, the owner with no eye for vintage Gibsons, the body battered and scratched, its rosewood fingerboard, a pair of Dirty Fingers. The guy taking a hundred bucks, throwing in a handful of picks and a soft case. Frankie pulled a page from *Punk* or some underground rag and hung it on her wall, a shot of Steve Jones playing one just like it. Teaching herself to play, doing it every chance she could ever since.

Rattling off a Junior Parker riff, she played around and took it into some Wanda Jackson, adding bends and vibrato.

Reaching the bottle of vodka from the freezer, Rita poured a shot in her bowl, Danone with chilled Absolut, saying, "You want some, sweetie?"

Frankie nodded, said thanks.

Rita poured it, bringing both bowls.

Sliding the V between her feet, Frankie took the bowl and said, "Thought you were easing up on the sauce?"

"Yeah, why I switched to vodka," Rita said, giving her a wink. Dipping a spoon, Rita sat on the opposite arm, saying, "All the flavors these guys put out, why not vodka on the bottom?"

"It's good." Frankie tipped her bowl, spooning boozy yogurt, telling Rita to write them, make a suggestion. The two of them laughing, then sitting quiet, finishing their yogurt. Frankie thinking of Marty's farm out on Zero Avenue, bottom end of Surrey, letting Waves of Nausea rehearse in the barn. Out in the middle of nowhere, nothing but miles of corn.

It was a long drive, but they could crank it as loud as they wanted, finding their sound. Frankie hooking her Flying V through the Univox Super-Fuzz and Alamo Futura Reverb. Tweaking that tube distortion, getting the sound creamy and thick. The power cords running through a snake, coming off a generator right outside the barn door.

The two guys Marty kept down there, Tucker and Sticky, were his eyes on the pot fields, packing up illegal dexies, stepping on coke and meth, making hash from trims and leaves. And whatever else Marty was into. Like a drug warehouse.

Friday nights, she'd been running her old Karmann Ghia out to the barn. Arnie Binz and Joey "Thunder" Rhoades packing their gear in back of Joey's mom's Ford wagon: drum kit, amp and Fender bass in back. The three of them setting up and grinding it out on the sawdust floor. Frankie punking that rockabilly sound, taking it a mile from old school, feeling their sound getting tight. Waves of Nausea ready to cut the EP, a real one, a big step up from the home-made tapes she'd been recording on her portable Philips, the one she toted around in her bag. The three of them listening to those tapes over and over, tweaking their sound.

All of them eager since this guy, Bud Luxford, came in Falco's one night, talking about putting together a compila-tion of Vancouver punk, said he wanted them on the record. The Waves excited about it, what with the Sticks putting out their third single, and D.O.A. set to release *Triumph of the Ignoroids*.

She'd been doing the booking for the Waves, getting them into any place she could, putting up her own money when she had any, taking care of any liquor permits, rental gear, whatever it took. Getting them into places like the Acadian and Odd Fellows, on bills with other emerging bands: Big Muff, Middle Finger, Infected, Ergot Fungus and Kiss the Carpet. Frankie living for the times like when they opened for U-J3RK5, or sitting in with the Generators, meeting guys like Buck Cherry and Harry Homo. Jamming with the Modernettes one night, back in the Active Dog days, switching guitars with Buck, him playing her Flying V, Frankie playing his beat-up SG.

Got to know Art and Barry the night the K-Tels did their Valentine's Day Massacre show at O'Hara's, back in February, passing joints and a jug of wine and talking about bands they loved. Buck introducing her to the guys from Sparkling Apple, the band calling their sound drunk-rock. Those guys inviting the Waves to a party at the Cave, living up to their drunken reputation, the Waves showing they could hold their own.

Joey Shithead had come out one night, catching the Waves at the Japanese Hall, saying she kicked ass, hot like that Poison Ivy chick from the Cramps. Frankie with the Flying V strapped on low, that wide-legged stance, wailing into the mic, hammering power chords. Didn't matter Arnie was on bass, Joey doing his Keith Moon rolls. Shithead saying she was the show, could have done it solo. Told her to get a hold of Gary Taylor and get her band booked into the Rock Room. Put her in touch with the guy who booked out the Ukranian Club over in Burnaby.

When the Waves got to rehearse down on Zero Avenue, the two guys working for Marty Sayles, Tucker and Sticky, stood at the side of the barn, leaning on the boards, no appreciation for the sound, their eyes glued on Frankie, the girl in tight denim, whipping her hair and jumping around. Tucker calling it crotch rock, knowing the girl was hands-off on account of the thing with Marty.

"What about the barn?" Rita said, pulling Frankie from her thoughts, like she was reading her mind.

Frankie made a sour face, saying she likely screwed that up.

"This Johnny's got a stage, right?" Rita said, guessing how Frankie felt, the way she talked about him. "Maybe something you two can work out."

"Yeah, maybe." Frankie smiling, spooning Absolut with Danone, saying, "But no way I'm cleaning his toilets." Laughing, saying, "You got to see it."

"No, thank you." Rita glanced at the clock again, sighed and went and splashed in more vodka, offered Frankie some.

Frankie shook her head, thinking she could look into this fifth-floor warehouse space a couple of the bands had been using for rehearsal. Right in town. The place was set to be demoed but still had electricity. Top of losing her rehearsal space, breaking it off with Marty meant she was out of work. No more picking up dope by the gym bag from Zero Avenue, taking it to Chop Suzy's and Euphoria's Top Floor, or hiding packets under her spare tire and running it across the border.

"Could teach guitar," Rita said, dipping her spoon, getting the last of it. "Do it right here if you want."

"That or find a club, one that'll let me swing round a pole."

"You're five years past L.A., remember? Whatever that means."

The two of them laughing some more, Rita joking about sticking tassels on her titties, telling Frankie things would work out. Getting up, she took Frankie's bowl, setting them in the sink, saying, "Got to hit the hay, kid, got an early day. You should, too."

"Yeah."

Too late to catch Carson. Frankie knowing if she lay down, she'd just stare at the ceiling, thinking shitty thoughts like not having a gig lined up till the one at Viking Hall, two weeks away, the three of them splitting a hundred bucks. The last gig had been at the Concourse, sharing the stage with Big Muff, a Blue Cheer knock-off band, both bands chipping in for the damage deposit, the management rolling out cheap carpet to save the hardwood underneath. The fans loving the show, but going crazy, ripping down the ceiling tiles and exit signs, leaving about a thousand burn holes and stains on the rolled-out carpet. The bands losing their deposit, but gaining some fans.

Rita's door closed, and Frankie took up her Flying V again and ran a G scale, unplugged, turning it into that old Count Five riff, "Psychotic Reaction," a G-major/F-major shuffle. Telling herself things would work out.

●

WAKING STIFF on the floor, the TV playing static, a bunch of guys on his floor, their amps, drum kit and gear stacked along the bar, everybody laid out in sleeping bags, the dog stretched out by the door. The Coors clock telling him it was nearly five in the morning, headache settling in like a fog, body feeling like both Holmes and Shavers pummeled the shit out of him.

Could go and knock on Arnie's door. Take him with to raid the pot field, get him to help stuff some bags. Arnie the kind of guy who liked the edge, plus he knew the area. But Johnny thought better of it, Arnie being Frankie's bass player. Decided to do this one solo, sure he'd feel better after pouring some coffee into himself.

Taking the Norton from a shelf below the register, the .22 pocket pistol he kept just in case. Johnny took the keys Art had left on the bar, stepped past the snoring dog and went out the front, looking at the mural van, thinking Jesus Christ. At least if Marty Sayles's guys spotted the van, Middle Finger would be long gone down the coast.

The van smelled of feet and dog, Johnny having to drive with his window down. Tanked her up at the all-night Esso. East Hastings was dead that time of morning, Johnny stopping again before the PNE, a place called the Last Drop, waffles twenty-four seven. The takeout double eased his head as he rolled east on the Number One. Down to cold dregs as he crossed the top of Surrey, checking Monk's map, taking the 176 south, past Fraser Downs, cutting across Eighth at the golf course, then south on the townline, gravel crunching under the van's wheels. He tossed the takeout cup to the passenger floor. Asking the guy in the rearview if he was up for this.

Headlights off, he pulled to the shoulder, Zero Avenue just ahead at the T intersection. The top of a silo in the distance, a windmill with a weathervane. Taking the Norton from under the seat, he slipped it in his pocket, giving a last glance at the rearview. Grabbing a handful of Glad bags from the box on the passenger seat, he stepped around back of the van. Looking at the swaying corn on both sides of the road. The sky to the east just starting to get light.

. . . LIVE FAST, DIE YOUNG

HARD TO forget the feel of getting shot with rock salt, stings like a bitch. That time in the Comox Valley on Vancouver Island, some backcountry pot-growing operation in the woods. Johnny hearing about it from some stripper at the Cecil. Got that tip for free. Taking the ferry over, he drove north from Nanaimo, found the rutted access road nobody had used in like a decade. Beat the hell out of the Scout's suspension finding the spot, all ruts and rocks. Then rolling up on about two hundred plants scattered in a clearing. Getting out, Johnny started bagging it up. Leaving the bags as he filled them, snipping off mostly tops.

Hearing someone coming through the trees, Johnny grabbed a couple of bags, getting chased by a pair of laid-off loggers and their mastiff, the fuckers yelling and cursing, half of it in German. Johnny swatting a sack at the snarling dog, the thing baring teeth like spikes, grabbing hold and tearing the bag wide open, the pot flying out. The blast from a twelve gauge and Johnny felt the rock salt, dropping the other bag and jumping in his Scout. Grabbing his Norton from under the seat, he cranked the window and returned fire, tramping the pedal and slinging gravel off his tires. The logger with the shotgun firing again, spitting curses, making his point with Sifto. Johnny not wanting to relive the experience, knowing Marty Sayles would have extra eyes down here this close to harvest, the reason he kept the pistol in his pocket. Walking the ditch now, he climbed the fence rail, swiping his way through the corn, the tassels over his head. Forgetting his hangover, he walked in about a hundred feet, a rooster crowing somewhere.

"Hope you got this one right, Falco." Parting the corn stalks, wet with dew, he stepped between the rows, careful where he set his feet on the loamy soil.

The way Monk had explained it, Marty Sayles's guys started these guerilla grows after the spring thaw, taking out double rows of foot-high corn and planting in their juvenile pot, doing it at night, keeping it well back from any roads, taking advantage of any irrigation systems in place. Letting the local farmers know they were doing it, going right to their doors and explaining the chance of a barn fire in case the law was called, or if the plants were sprayed with Roundup, shit like that.

Marty's guys coming back at harvest time, the plants reaching five or six feet tall and bushy as Christmas trees. Crashing their pickups through the corn at night, picking under the headlight beams and hauling it out. Monk telling him Marty's fields dotted all along the Fraser Valley. Over a dozen farms. Farmers turning a blind eye, nobody saying a word.

Johnny wishing he had maps for all of them, guessing Monk and Stain would be doing this themselves, except the

Hellrazors couldn't afford any trouble with Marty Sayles. Not after half the charter had been run off or hospitalized after the all-night bash at the clubhouse, raided by local dads looking for their teenaged daughters. Johnny overhearing Stain and Monk talking about patching over, both of them shaking their heads, embarrassed about it.

Wading through the leaves slapping dew at his denim now, Johnny looked at the corn tassels turning brown, cobs swelling and ready to pick. Shivering from the morning damp, he parted more leaves and moved through the stalks, the rows three feet apart.

Then there it was. Pot plants, fat and bushy, the larger leaves a nice yellowy brown, the stigmas starting to wither, buds just losing that rich green color. Ready to pick.

Flapping open a bag, Johnny set to work with the pruners, cutting the tops and upper branches, working from plant to plant, leaving a filled bag and stuffing the next one. Taking care of the back rent, thinking about the bands he could hire next month, how he could stuff his back room with cases of beer.

Rustling to his right had him ducking. Listening. Touching the pistol in his pocket, he stayed in a crouch. Definitely something pushing through the corn ahead of him. Johnny's heart thumping. The cornstalks felt like walls closing in around him.

Waiting. Feeling that rock-salt burn again. Ready to run the hell out of there, but he forced himself to stay like that, five minutes feeling like an hour. Finally telling himself it was a deer or the breeze pushing the tassels. Whatever it was, it was gone.

Tucking away the pistol, he flapped out another bag and snipped more tops, shoving them in. Filling a dozen bags, he grabbed two at a time and made his way back to the fence, going back for the rest and lining them all up. Checking for anybody on the road, he tossed them in the back of the van, plush carpeting on the floor, inside panels and ceiling padded with Naugahyde. A brass plaque screwed into the shag declared it *the shagging wagon*.

Making a three-point turn on the gravel, he got the hell out of there, driving back the way he came. More than enough in back for some breathing room. And getting out of there without being spotted meant he'd go right on breathing.

Johnny grinning at the guy in the rearview, saying, "I told you," switching on the radio. Blondie doing "Denis."

Doo be do.

Johnny feeling on top of things, getting out from under the back rent, thinking of Frankie del Rey again as he got back on the Number One, heading toward to the city, careful to keep it to the speed limit. Johnny still trying to get used to the highway signs in kilometers, the old van's speedometer set in miles.

. . . SAY IT WITH FLOWERS

"THE HELL you expect?" Zeke Chamas said.

Frankie del Rey stood there grinning at him.

Hair like a flokati rug, looking ill without all the heavy eye make-up. The girl not wearing a bra as far as he could tell. The Sex Pistols T-shirt, a men's extra large, fitting her like a dress. Her legs pale, her toenails painted black.

Never got what Marty saw in this chick. Zeke betting she had fur under her armpits, thinking Marty was losing his grip to the booze and the marching powder. Marty doing more and more lines all the time, snorting it up, riding around in back while Zeke played the chauffeur.

After the beating Zeke put on the guy at Lubik's, Marty helped himself to some of the poppers from the guy's bag. Told Zeke it made sex something else. Marty telling Zeke to drive him to Falco's club last night, the man riding in back, high as a kite. Seeing about the back rent and collecting from some chick dealer, meeting her there. Didn't say it was a blow job he was collecting. Said he was taking Frankie for some Italian, then back to his place for some French, whatever that meant. Frankie spoiled it by walking in on Marty and the chick and knocking the chick out. Zeke losing respect for the man, thinking about quitting, but then Marty said when he got his license back, he was taking himself off the front line and putting Zeke in charge, seeing what he could do.

Marty called up this morning, Zeke thinking this was it, but instead, Marty sent him to some florist's, then to Frankie's place with a fistful of flowers. This chick holding some kind of hoodoo over the man.

"He's letting things slide," Zeke said. "Not making a thing about what you pulled."

"What I pulled . . . you mean the thing with Marty and the blonde, one with his cock in her mouth." Frankie liked how Zeke flushed and looked away.

"Is what it is," he said, hating this. Wanting to backhand her into place.

"So he's saying it with flowers, huh?"

Holding them out like he was choking the bouquet, roses, a dozen in red.

"Asked me to do it as a favor, so I'm fucking doing it." Zeke shaking the flowers. "Here."

"Just doing what you're told, huh, Zeke?" Frankie taking them, enjoying this guy, letting the door rest on her hip.

He wanted to belt her, knock her on her ass. Looking to the elevator, Zeke rolled his tongue inside his cheek, pulled himself together, tried again, saying, "Got a card. Ought to read it."

"Yeah, you write it?" She looked at it. A printed verse, somebody signing Marty's name. Roses wrapped in tissue and tied with raffia, a nice gold seal. Didn't come from Safeway — at least that.

"I were you, I'd stop busting my balls, you understand me?"

Sniffing the bouquet, Frankie wondered how this guy got into the building without her buzzing him in, saying, "Yeah, sure, Zeke, the thought that counts, right?" Frankie guessed his momma dropped him on his head, more than just the one time.

Man, he wanted to hit her. Zeke saying, "I were you, I'd call him up, try and make amends."

"Do like I'm told, huh? Doesn't matter the guy's an ass-hole?"

"You can think it, just don't say it," Zeke said, starting to turn for the elevator now. "And when you're thinking it, smile like hell, and tell yourself you don't mean it."

"You mean kiss his ass, huh?"

"Take it any way you want. And, oh, he gets his license back, gonna be driving himself around."

"Yeah, so?"

"So, he's putting me in charge."

"No shit? Good for you."

"Meaning you answer to me." He let that sink in, then said, "Best get them in water." Turning for the elevator. "I got shit to do."

"Dropping more flowers?"

Waving a finger, Zeke shook his head, but smiling now.

Putting her nose to the blooms again, she said, "Tell him thanks."

"Tell him yourself." Zeke pressed the button, the elevator pinged, the door opened and he stepped in.

Hearing the elevator going down, she closed the door and slid on the chain.

Rita calling from down the hall, "He gone, hon?"

"Yeah."

Stepping from the bathroom, Rita rubbed her hair with a towel, looking at the flowers but not saying anything, coming into the kitchen. Frankie smelling the Agree shampoo, Rita stopping the greasies. She laid the bouquet on the counter.

"Roses, huh?"

"Yeah."

"How about breakfast?" Rita said.

"Just yogurt, no vodka." Frankie wishing she had some of that bhang left, saying, "We got anything like a vase?"

. . . THE REBEL KIND

JOHNNY SAT on the stool, his arms on the bar, the closed sign hanging on the front door. Taking the .22, he pulled the clip. Hadn't fired it since that time in the Comox Valley, not sure he could do it, point it at a man and shoot. Just like that. Replacing the clip, he put it under the bar, snapped a cap and swallowed some beer, his thumb scraping the label. Looking at Murphy's number written on the slip of paper: Monk saying the guy would take the weed off his hands, not caring where it came from.

It was Frankie he wanted to call, more about a date than a gig. Looking up when Arnie's key scraped the lock. Arnie coming through the door, old T-shirt with slopped paint and torn-up jeans, his bass slung over a shoulder, amp in hand, asking, "Need me today?"

Johnny saying, "Tonight, and we open at eight." Arnie was always late.

Waving a hand, walking by the bar, Arnie reminded him it was his night off. He had a practice tonight and was just locking his gear in back till later if that was alright.

"Something wrong with your place?"

"You kidding? Some fucker jimmied my shit lock. Took my stash of cash, looking around for drugs. Super said he'd get around to fixing it."

Johnny said just till tonight, he needed the room for beer, watching Arnie breeze out the door, leaving it unlocked.

Tapping the Rothman's pack, he pulled out a smoke, fishing for his lighter. He reached for the phone, making the call to Murphy. The phone rang as his hand touched the receiver, Zeke Chamas on the other end, saying, "You got something for me?"

"Who's this?" Johnny drew on the cigarette, waiting, knowing who it was.

Zeke saying his name.

"The driver?"

"Now I'm the guy collecting." Zeke jumping the gun, wanting to show Marty some initiative.

Johnny waited.

"Look, play all the fag music you want," Zeke said, "but the rent's the rent. Want what you owe."

"Like I told Marty —"

"That's not going to fly with me, you haven't got it, then you're out the door."

"Like I told him, I'm scraping it up." Johnny blew a smoke ring. "Might have half later." Give Johnny time to connect with Murphy, then make a beer run, fill the back of the Scout with two-fours, cans this time after what happened the other night.

"I got to come to you, I'm tacking on two points," Zeke told him.

"We open at eight." Johnny hung up. Smiling. Might be fun watching Zeke walk in with Stain at the door.

Across the street, the old rummy who came in last night steadied himself against a shopping cart filled with empties and plastic bags, staggering to the wall of the used book shop, undoing his pants and urinating on the bricks, spraying left and right like he was painting. Middle of the day, cars driving back and forth. Down here, nobody paid much attention.

Johnny glad he wasn't that guy, the phone ringing again, Johnny guessing Zeke thought of a smooth comeback. Lifting the receiver, Johnny found himself talking to Jade Blade, the girl telling him her drummer just came down with a nasty bug, the Dishrags having to cancel the weekend, telling him sorry, hoping to do it another time. Leaving him without a band.

Hanging up, he looked back out the front, the old guy shoving his cart, his piss staining the wall. Johnny sighing, dialing Murphy's number.

. . . SWITCHBACK

A POCKED face and a discount haircut, Murphy floated in the cord jacket, his polo shirt tucked over a middle going soft. The two of them in the alley, back of Johnny's Omaha-orange Scout, bags of weed stuffed in back, on the rear bench, on the passenger seat and floor. Murphy's Econoline blocked the mouth of the alley, its four-ways flashing, making it look like a delivery, keeping their business private.

"Asking two-fifty a bag." The price Monk had told him. Johnny watching Murphy lift the tarp, checking inside one of the Glad bags, taking a handful of flower top, checking for mold, giving it a sniff.

"Ought to hear the shit I ask for," Murphy said. "I can go eighty a bag."

"You kidding me?"

Murphy saying the only reason they were even talking, one of his guys got busted crossing the border last week, half mile from the farm on Zero Avenue, middle of the night. The Mounties working a sting with Washington state troopers, catching his guy with a rucksack of bricks and bhang. Only good thing that came out of it, his guy was stand-up and wasn't talking to the cops, taking the heat, staring at a couple years.

"How about two even?" Johnny said.

"No can do, man. Eighty's doing you a favor."

"Some favor. Come on, it's quality, most of it flower tops."

"You got somebody else, call 'em up. Me, I can pretty much guess the source. So I got some exposure here."

"Sounds like a bunch of shit."

"You want the eighty or not?"

"Make it a hundred then, and it's yours." Johnny thinking, like, what choice did he have?

Murphy making a show out of it, saying yeah, he'd take it.

Counting out the bills, Murphy slapped twelve hundred in his hand, saying, "How about a hand?" Murphy slid open the van's side door, went around back of the Scout, tugging a bag in each fist, tossing them in the van. Johnny grabbing a bag, wanting it done.

When he climbed behind the wheel, Murphy rolled down the window, saying, "You get any more, maybe I can do better." Flicking off his four-ways, Murphy put her in reverse, then turned onto Hastings and was gone.

It was enough for the back-rent and next month's, a beer run or two, and it would allow him to book a few acts. He was back to thinking about Zeke Chamas coming to pick up the rent, Stain making him pay the cover, both ways. Got him smiling, walking in the back door, remembering he was stuck without a band for the weekend. Went and tried Frankie's number, getting her machine, her aunt's voice telling him to leave a message. He'd try again after the beer run.

He'd been scraping by on illegal beer sales since he

opened the club eight months back. Had finally got together the cash for the liquor license, made enough to pay Stain to watch the door, giving a heads-up anytime the cops showed up, everybody underage knowing to hide their beer, the volume getting turned down. The deposit on the place, the bar and the awning out front had taken most of his savings. Johnny had been turned down by every bank in town, his dream of turning Falco's Nest into a west-coast CBGB getting kicked at every turn.

The building was a rat trap like most of them down here, but the location was good, Falco's catching the runoff from the Smilin' Buddha up the block. He'd gone up to meet Lachman when he first opened, asked the man how he did it, putting punk on the Vancouver map, shaking that No Fun City image and making a buck at the same time. Lachman sat at his chessboard and pointed to his wife behind the bar, said it was all her. He and Johnny hitting it off. Still went up to see Lachman now and then, play a little chess. Have a beer with Igor, the Yugoslavian doorman. Johnny asking about the time Lachman kicked out Hendrix. Lachman rolling his eyes, moving his rook, still trying to live that one down.

Johnny reached into the cooler now, popped a cap and swallowed some beer, an idea coming to him. Why not rob Marty Sayles again, guessing his crew would harvest the pot from all the fields, cure it all at one time, do it in that barn down on Zero Avenue.

. . . NO PLAN

ZEKE HAD called her up and told her Marty just bumped him up. Frankie asking if it hurt. Getting pissed, Zeke asked if she wanted to keep fucking around or get to work. Frankie said she was sorry, Zeke telling her to get her pasty ass over to Suzy's, be a bag waiting, then he hung up.

Pasty ass.

Zeke wasn't the chauffeur delivering flowers anymore. Just like that.

A good buzz from the black hash she copped off Stain, Frankie walked in the door of the haircut joint on Guildford. The slogan in Chop Suzy's window promised you come in a train wreck, you go out a goddess. Looking like Farrah Fawcett or Dorothy Hamill. A poster of Jane Fonda in a two-piece, straddling a chair, curls from *Coming Home* blowing, looking happy to be alive. A poster in the other window of Stefanie Powers, looking hot on the set of *Hart to Hart*. A decal by the cash read *we do brides.*

She'd been thinking of having hers lopped shorter, give it some spikes with Dippity-do. Could work. Breezing in, Frankie said hey to the girls cutting hair, three of the chairs with customers. Going to the office in back, making the pickup from Suzy. Suzy good with the snips, putting on the French accent, making small talk. The woman who claimed she studied under Vidal. Not so good with her choice of business partners though. Marty Sayles stepping in and bailing her out two years ago, saving her from ruin, the woman in debt all the way to her black roots. Marty injecting enough cash to clear the stack of overdue notices off her desk, give the place a pulse and put in the fifth chair. Suzy able to hire a couple of decent cutters, turning the place around. Booked solid weeks in advance now. Doing alright for a strip mall in Surrey. Across from a Dollar Store. Running regular ads in the *Sun*. Marty owning one-third, using Suzy's as a drop, laundering his cash through the books.

Chitchat she'd picked up from the girls with the snips: Marty had a thing for Suzy, going back to the days before the drugs and the bimbos on their knees. The man still came creeping now and then when he wasn't too high, but always after hours.

Frankie walked back out to the parking lot, acting like she had all day, the pink sports bag with *Gee Your Hair Smells Terrific* printed on the side, swinging from her shoulder, looked like Barbie designed it. Dexies packed inside shampoo bottles. Dropping it on the passenger seat of her Karmann Ghia, enough pills to get her three to five in Corrections, she popped in the lighter and dropped another piece of hash on it, toking as she drove out of there, popping a cassette in the player, "Cretin Hop" rattling the speakers. Frankie singing along.

Watching her speed now, she took the 152 up to the

highway, slowing on the ramp. High enough to take off the edge, she was starting to hate these guys. Zeke and Marty in equal measure. No idea why Zeke had her running sport bags across town, Marty only had her making runs across the Peace Arch, timed it right, paying a border guard named Palmer to look the other way. Frankie making the drops to Murphy in Birch Bay, his trailer at the back of some RV park. A barbecue and a couple of lawn chairs out front.

It didn't matter. A few more runs and she'd have enough to cut the EP. Hoping her heap held out, the Karmann Ghia shaking like it was suffering, tires with worn treads, three of them whitewalls, the fourth one in back not matching.

Walking onto the used car lot last March, Frankie checked out the cars and got sucked in by the fresh coat of Zambezi green. The salesman's blue eyes clinched the deal, the guy named Norm pointed out the low mileage, pitched her on butt-welded panels, the air-cooled flat four with the dual Solex carbs. May as well have been talking Greek. Frankie signed where he pointed and drove it home. Norm throwing in a set of floor mats. All the car she could afford.

Rita was the first to kick the tires, pointing out the Bondo, the lower part of the rear fender looking like it had been smeared on with a putty knife. A hole where the aerial used to be. Wiper blade held on with a shoelace. Frankie hadn't seen any of that past the blue eyes and green paint, made like none of it bothered her, saying the scars added character. Top of that it came with the aftermarket Craig tape player, the kind that slid out on a bracket, Pioneer speakers, too.

Joey Ramone was pouring through the speakers now,

singing about his momma being on pills and the baby having the chills. Side A ended, and Frankie dug in the glove box, swapping tapes. Siggy Magic's "Tooth Decay" playing, Frankie pulling off at Grandview, passing some orange four-by-four, the guy looking over, dark shades and a knit beanie. Heading back to town, she was making this drop at Euphoria's Top Floor, another place Marty had a stake in, over on Commercial. Zeke told her to trade the pink bag for a bag of cash, then bring it to him, waiting at Mitchell's garage, down off Boundary at Marine.

So Zeke was running the show, Marty Sayles insulating himself. Tooting too much coke and losing focus. Marty setting up a tanning salon on Robson. Drug money buying a bunch of tanning beds with high-tech lamps invented by some German. Twenty bulbs pumping out a hundred watts, mimicking the sun's own rays. Marty having them shipped across the Atlantic, calling the new place Endless Summer. The bronze mirage package promising a tan all year, save customers a trip to the Mexican sun, what with the uv rays and all them *cucarachas* down there. His Down South option offered spray-on sun. Forty bucks a month and Marty's girls airbrushed on a tan, darkening the natural pigments without any sun or lamps. Told Frankie all about it over their first dinner, Marty showing her who he was, Frankie smiling, trying to look interested.

Had to give him credit though, the guy knew how to turn a buck, just smelled an opportunity. But as far as women went, Marty didn't have a fucking clue.

The shimmy started again from the front end, Frankie rolling along Grandview, letting up on the pedal until the shimmy went away. Maybe she'd get it looked at over at Mitchell's. Bobby the mechanic, a guy she met at the WISE Hall, told her he could fix her up with a set of Goodyears at cost. Frankie saying she'd think about it, never returning his calls, guessing she'd be paying retail now.

Good thing Rita had the spare room, the condo on Victoria, let Frankie stay as long as she wanted, her aunt pretty cool for someone in her forties. Frankie always insisting on kicking in something for the bills. Rita never taking it. It sure beat living in some roach dive, Frankie thinking of the dilapidated place over on Gore where D.O.A. used to crash. Chuck Biscuits telling her about the time he woke and a silverfish crawled from his ear, the tickling feeling freaked him out.

Back when he was huffing cooking spray, Arnie Binz had crashed for a week inside a giant cardboard carton, the kind used for shipping a freezer. Told her it wasn't so bad, the cardboard thick enough to block most of the rain, just his sneakers getting wet — room for Arnie and his Thunderbird bass. Worked fine till the garbage truck rolled down the lane, making its regular pick-up. Arnie waking in time to grab his bass and roll out, the trash man ramming his forks through the cardboard. Man and Gibson spared. Arnie went on to sleep in his gypsy cab for a time, not like he could afford a room at the Cobalt or the Roosevelt. Finally succumbing to employment, landing a job at a 7-Eleven, getting promptly canned, then lucking into the part-time hours at Falco's, Johnny paying minimum wage but treating him alright. Arnie making the best of it, showing up for his shift most of the time. Got himself the flop on the third floor and had been living there ever since. Straightening himself out.

Switching to the outside lane now, passing cars, Frankie tapped her hands on top of the wheel. Frankie lending harmonies to "Passive and Blue," glancing at the rearview as she rolled along.

That's when she saw it, the lyrics catching in her throat. The same orange four-by-four a few cars back. Pretty sure it had been there all the way across Grandview, staying a couple of cars back. Gave her a bad feeling. The driver, with shades and a knit beanie, had the Serpico look. Frankie's heart hammered. Sure it was a narc, seeing herself facing three to five. He pulled around the cars between them, started waving to her.

Shit.

Stepping on the gas, forgetting the shimmy, Frankie ran an amber light going to red, trying to shake him.

. . . PROBABLE CAUSE

THOUGHT SHE lost him, then there he was again — Serpico
— three cars back, putting on his signal, waving at her.
Frankie too high for this.

Switching lanes again, she swung the Ghia up Nanaimo,
sped up and got onto Broadway, weaving in and out of
traffic, nearly creamed a vw bug. Somebody honking. No
way she was getting pulled over with the pink bag full of
pills, end up thrown into Lakeside Correctional. No music
career in a place like that.

Eyes on the mirror, she wheeled another turn and pulled
into a Shell on the corner, stopped by the pump and cranked
down the window. Looking at the station's plate glass, she
checked the distorted reflections of the cars going by. Not
sure what to do, ready to chuck the bag, run if she had
to. Could abandon her car, call it in stolen. Grabbing her
handbag and the pink bag, she stepped to the island, a bag
hanging from each shoulder, standing by the trash disposal.
Ready to shove the pink bag in the trash, say what fucking
bag. Taking the nozzle, smelling gas fumes.

"I got it." The attendant came from behind, made her jump, pointing to the full-serve sign.

Frankie looked at him, saying, "What?"

"This one's full serve, Miss."

Frankie taking a second, understanding what he meant, saying, "Yeah, sorry, got my mind on, you know . . . things."

"Sure, how much you want?"

"What?"

"Gas, Miss, how much?"

"Oh, I don't know . . . like ten bucks, I guess." Giving up the nozzle, eyes glancing at the road. She asked for the rest room key, thinking she could flush the pills if she had to. The attendant telling her it was hanging from a hook inside.

"Leaded or unleaded?" he called after her.

"What?"

"This one's extra unleaded." Pointing to the blue pump she'd pulled up to.

"Uh . . . yeah, whatever you think's best."

"How about the oil, check that, too?"

"That'd be great. How about a phone, you got one of those?"

Pointing around the side, the guy thinking people were getting stranger by the day, watching this girl with the two bags go inside for the key, still looking when she came back out.

She went to the can, locked the door, shoved the pink bag in the trash can, splashed cold water on her face. Pulling paper towel from the dispenser, she dried herself and balled it on top of the pink bag. Fishing a dime from the bottom of her handbag, she went out and picked up the receiver, dropped in the coin, heard the clink, then the tone, then dialed and waited, saying, "Zeke, yeah, think we got a problem."

"Yeah, what now?"

"Think I got a tail."

"A what? What d'ya mean, you think? Fuck, where are you?"

"Ah . . . on Nanaimo . . . no, Commercial. Stopped for gas. Shell, I think. Maybe Esso."

"Okay, take it easy, shit . . . so, what about this tail."

"I don't know, a van or one of those . . ." Frankie waving her hands, saying, "Guy with shades on, waving at me, wanting me to pull over. Was behind me since . . . like forever."

"Okay, where's he now?"

"Don't know, might've lost him. I'm around the side of the pumps, dumped the bag in the can. No way I'm —"

"Hey, hey, you're on a phone."

"Right."

"And no way you're not dumping nothing."

"Hey, I'm not getting —"

"Said not on the phone. 'Sides, you want to try explain it to Marty . . . after all the shit you been pulling . . ." Zeke letting it sink in.

Frankie thinking which would be worse, getting busted or facing Marty. Watching a lady come around the side, her *Charlie's Angels* hair bouncing, going to the washroom door and rattling the knob, looking at her by the phone, the washroom key tag in her hand, calling to her, "You done, Miss?"

"Just a second?"

Zeke saying, "What's going on?"

"Some lady, asking me for the key to the can."

"So, give it to her."

"The stuff's in there, the bag, I stuffed it in the trash can. Not sure what to do."

"Fuckin' go get it. Jesus."

Frankie left the phone dangling, going to the door, using the key, telling the woman something was repeating. "Be just a sec." Going in, the door shutting behind her, taking the bag from the trash, going out, holding the key up for Charlie's Angel, telling her to have a nice day, going back to the phone.

"Here's what you do," Zeke said, "One, you calm the hell down, get the bag and stick it in the trunk. Two, you roll down Commercial, go past that Italian joint, place you were supposed to have dinner, you got me?"

"Think so, yeah."

Zeke giving her some left and right directions, then said, "You stop past the school. Know where I mean?"

"Think so."

"You park and wait till I get there."

"I don't know, Zeke . . ."

"Don't need to know. Why I'm telling you. And Frankie?"

"Yeah?"

"You better have that bag." Zeke saying he was on his way, then hanging up.

The attendant dropped the squeegee in the bucket of blue, watching her come around the side, saying, "The oil's a bit low, but still okay, but your tires . . ." He pointed, shaking his head.

"Yeah, I know." Handing him her Shell card, she said

something about living dangerously, then fished her keys from her pocket, dropped both bags inside on the far seat, shooting a nervous look around. Waiting for the guy to go swipe her card and come back, handing her the card, pointing a greasy finger at the imprinter, showing her where to sign, telling her to press hard.

Taking her copy, she got in and tossed her card and receipt in her bag. Charlie's Angel coming out of the can, looking at her, her Mercedes coupe at the far pump, the attendant pumping in the extra unleaded. Sticking in her key, Frankie started her car, worked the shift and rolled back onto Commercial. Sticking in another cassette, she turned it up.

Damned Damned Damned.

Hoping the music would ease her nerves.

Passing the Italian joint, Paesano's, the place Marty wanted to take her to dinner, night she clocked the blonde. Everything slow-cooked and homemade, mozzarella and olives shipped from the old country. Espresso done right. Cannoli to die for.

Bopping to "Fan Club" now, she licked somebody else's tongue around her mouth, her nerves still shot. Frankie thinking she could use a chunk of bhang. Her eyes on the rearview, keeping watch for the four-by-four, Serpico with the shades and beanie.

Past Pender, she stomped the brakes, some kid in a ball cap on backwards darted from behind a parked Buick, dashing across the lane, a paper bag in his hand. She yelled at him, sounding like somebody's mother, the kid flipping her the bird, Frankie flipping it back.

Making a right, she ground the shifter, getting caught behind a delivery van, a big square box with a rusty bumper, coming to a stop. Her engine stalled in the lane, Frankie checking the rearview, no sign of Serpico.

The delivery van's four-ways flashed on, and the driver climbed out, coming around the back, waving her around, giving her some courtesy.

Turning the key, she rolled past the big box and took the next left. Pretty sure that's what Zeke told her. Cars were parked on either side of the tree-lined road, she felt like she was driving down a funnel.

Had to be an idiot, doing this, still running Marty's dope across town. Catching him with his pants down should have ended it, the guy saying she was five years past L.A., Zeke telling her to get her pasty ass down here.

She turned on Venables, to McLean. Williams to Cotton, then Charles. Nobody in the rearview as she rolled past the back of the schoolyard. Young kids playing at recess, boys bouncing basketballs, the shrill of schoolgirls, teachers standing like prison guards. Turning her head back to the road, she hit the brakes.

Serpico in the orange ride was practically blocking the road, hanging his arm out his window, waving to her like it was her move.

Fuck.

No way to hide the bag. Nowhere to go.

Serpico stepped out, left his door hanging open. Lighting a smoke, he walked up. Nearly halfway to her window before she recognized Johnny Falco. Never seen him outside the club in daylight, or with the shades and the beanie.

"Jesus Christ, Johnny." Hand to her chest.

Taking off the shades, he gave her a smile, hooked them on the neck of his jersey, saying, "You trying to duck me?"

"Scared me half to death."

Said he spotted her on the road while he was making his beer run, so he followed her, wanted to ask about playing Falco's this weekend. She wasn't really taking in what he was saying. Trying to lighten things, he said he figured she was just a shitty driver, running lights and being erratic, didn't know she was trying to evade him. He said he lost her back before the Shell. Johnny picking up a pack of smokes at the 7-Eleven, seeing her again when she made the turn off Commercial, Johnny hanging the next right, circling the block, hoping to catch her coming down the next street. Pointing to the *Gee Your Hair Smells Terrific* bag, he nodded and put it together, clapping his forehead, the booze and coke from last night making him slow, saying, "Thought you were done with Marty Sayles and all that. Oh, man, I'm real sorry."

"Fuck, that took years off, Johnny," Frankie said, her heart still pounding, saying, "So, you chased me down, just wanted to say howdy, that it?"

"Well, you put it like that . . ." he said, guessing it wasn't the best time to ask.

. . . JANIE JONES

"Nearly wet myself." Her heartbeat slowing, Frankie forcing a smile.

"Not what I was going for," he said, leaning on her window, offering her a smoke, saying, "Really figured me for a cop, huh? Pulling you over, asking for license and registration."

"Some guy follows me, with the shades, looking like that, yeah, a cop."

Taking a smoke from his pack, Rothman's not her usual brand. She let him light her up, cupping her hand over his, this guy with maybe a dozen years on her twenty-four, looking pleased with himself.

"You got one, right?" he asked.

"One what?

"A license."

"Yeah, well, I'm driving aren't I?"

"And a name, you got one of those, ma'am?" Trying to do Jack Webb, getting her to smile.

"Yeah, you can call me Janie Jones." Not sure why she

was smiling, switching tapes, getting out the D.O.A., saying, "Now what, you going to frisk me?"

"Been watching *Five*-o on the tube, huh, seeing how they do it?"

"Got better things to do with my prime time."

"After that thing in the can, thought you were all done with that." Johnny pointed at the gym bag.

"So, you ran me down. You said hello. And, here we are, middle of the road, me with a bag full of pills out front of a schoolyard. Something that'll double my sentence . . ."

"Right. Was making my beer run . . ." He looked around, saying, "You want to put her in park?" Johnny pointed to the shoulder, a willow with its branches hanging down.

"Can't park on a slope . . . hand brake's shot. So, how about you just spit it out?"

Johnny glanced down at her patched rear fender, the bald whitewalls. "Know it's short notice, but you got plans this weekend?"

"This you asking me out?"

"More like I need a band Friday and Saturday."

"What happened to the Dishrags?"

"Cancelled last minute. Leaves me in a bit of a jam, so I was hoping you'd help me out." Johnny saying it paid a hundred bucks a night.

Frankie not caring, jumping at the chance. A jumble of thoughts rushing through the hash haze: call up Joey Thunder and Arnie, some friends, sort out what to wear, stick a playlist together.

"So, what if it *was* like a date?"

"Well, I'm busy this weekend." Frankie beamed.

Pulling a smoke from his pack, he fished for his lighter and lit up. "So, am I forgiven for scaring the hell out of you?"

"Oh, shit!" she said.

"What?"

"Called Zeke, when I thought you were . . ." Telling him the short strokes about the phone call at the Shell, about Zeke saying he was on the way. "Gonna be here, like any minute."

A bell rang in the schoolyard, the kids started lining at the back door, ready to file inside, teachers waving their arms.

Dragging on the cigarette, Johnny took his time, looking up and down the street. The schoolyard starting to empty.

"You know Zeke carries a gun, right?"

"Yeah, some fellows need it." Johnny tapped the cigarette, ash falling, saying he'd catch her later, putting the shades back on, taking his time walking back to the Scout.

Frankie watched him go, smiling, this guy part Marlboro Man, part Serpico. Looking in her rearview, then up the street, stamping her butt in the ashtray. Johnny made a three-point turn and drove off. Spinning her story, she waited under the willow for Zeke's Nova to rumble down the car-lined street.

. . . SHOOT THE MOON

THE FOG settled low over the cornfield. Arnie Binz snapped off branches, grabbing weed by the handful, tossing it in the bag, stripping the lower branches, working fast like that, thinking there had to be at least a hundred plants between the rows of corn, the corn standing over his head. Somebody had been through ahead of him, taking mostly the tops. Arnie knowing it was Johnny. Footprints all over the soft earth. Thought he'd get his share before Marty's guys realized somebody had been through, picking their weed.

Moving along the row, Arnie broke off more and tossed handfuls in the sack. Hearing crows squawking nearby. Angling and working along, Arnie kept a sense of direction. Couldn't chance losing the way back to his Pinto, left it along the ditch, Arnie planning to fill the hatch and backseat of the Cruising Wagon, the one with the bubble windows and rainbow stripes.

One bag full, Arnie dropped it and worked along the row, stripping and tossing, when he heard it. Rustling, thinking it was the crows, he kept working, then came the voices.

Dropping down, he shoved the sack behind the row, moved back and tucked the other one under a plant.

Two guys talking, coming his way through the corn. Leaving the sacks, Arnie ducked low and angled through the rows, moving away, stopping and waiting, keeping track which way the car was. He'd get back out to the road, take off and come back later for the sacks. Feeling in his pocket for his keys. Not in his pocket. Arnie feeling the panic rise, then remembering he left them in the ignition to keep from losing them.

The voices were closer, Arnie stayed crouched down, keeping quiet. Could be Tucker and Sticky, the guys who worked the farm, guys he knew from the practice sessions, the two of them always standing around, listening, their eyes on Frankie. Moving between the rows, not wanting to explain what he was doing here. The practice not till tonight.

Arnie had overheard Monk talking to Johnny, saw him drawing the map. The field Arnie had told Monk about, half hoping Johnny would ask him to help him rip it off. Would have told Johnny where it was for free, Arnie knowing about Johnny's money troubles, guessing he came and ripped off Marty Sayles to save his club, pay the rent he owed the man.

Scrambling along the rows, he kept moving away from the voices, away from his car, too. Nearing the end of the corn, Arnie started to angle between the rows, moving back toward the road. He'd get out of there and walk back to the car, make like he was going for a walk in the fog, enjoying some autumn air. If they caught up with him, he'd say Frankie left a message, something about a practice, Arnie getting his a.m. mixed up with his p.m. Blame it on being high on the bhang these guys had been making.

The corn ended at a fallow field. Arnie able to see the townline from there.

"This way," a voice called, somebody crashing through the corn, getting close.

Moving along the edge of the field, Arnie kept low and threw a look over his shoulder, his foot hooking a dirt clod. Down he went, the wind knocked out of him. He started to push up.

Sticky, real name Lenny Lowe, stepped from the rows ahead of him, cutting him off. Looking surprised to see him.

"Scared the shit out me, man," Arnie said, thinking this guy wasn't much. Scrawny and unshaven and no gun in his belt. Sticky calling out, "Got him. Over here, Tuck."

"Hey, hey, no need for that. Just got myself turned around, man," Arnie said, walking up to the guy. "You know me." Swinging a fist, he put Sticky down, the smaller man clutching hold of Arnie's leg, yelling, "Tucker, get here!"

Couldn't walk with Sticky hanging on, Arnie punched down at him, trying to shake him off, Sticky ducked his head, refusing to let go.

Tucker Balco shoved his way through the stalks, the shotgun up like an oar, the big man swinging the butt.

An explosion against Arnie's skull, Arnie spinning into a dark hole.

Not sure if he blacked out. Aware of the two standing over him. Felt the pain in his head, blood trickling down his face, along his neck. Keeping his eyes closed.

"Momma teach you to fight like that?" Tucker said to Sticky.

"Fucking hung on, didn't I?"

"How about you just go make the call."

"What're we gonna do?"

"You're going to make the call."

"Why not you?"

Arnie heard the slap, opening his eyes, his right eye nearly swollen shut.

Tucker saying to Sticky, "On your way back, bring some rope."

Sticky going off, grumbling, doing like he was told, disappearing into the corn.

"Looks like you already been through once, huh?" Tucker asked, squatting next to Arnie, seeing he was awake now, standing the butt of the twelve gauge on the ground. "Golden rule, never go back." He bent and pulled a lace from his Nike.

"Got it wrong, man," Arnie said, looking through his one eye. "Was just cutting across, walking around. Know we got a jam tonight, right?"

The big man leaned the shotgun against a stalk, then flipped Arnie over on his stomach. Dropping a knee against his spine, he tied his hands with the lace. "Who's with you, Arnie?"

"Nobody, man."

Tucker tightened the lace, cinching it and grabbing some hair and tipping Arnie's head back, saying, "Guy that'll be coming, his name's Zeke. You know him?"

Arnie tried to nod.

"Guy driving Marty around, just got kicked up to hard-ass. Got something to prove." Tucker taking the lace from his other shoe, tying Arnie's ankles together. "Don't know why the fuck Marty keeps the guy around, but, the point is, he's gonna be asking you the same questions."

"Like I told you —"

Tucker swept his hand, slapping Arnie quiet, a welt that would show opposite the swollen eye. Tucker talking, "Heard he caught some guy at Lubik's, the guy being where he shouldn't be. Anyway, my point is, Zeke's someplace between attack dog and psycho, putting on a show for Marty to see." Tucker sat him up, saying, "So, you wanna do yourself a favor, talk to me while we're waiting. Go easier if you do." Tucker waited, but Arnie just sat looking at him through the one eye, Tucker saying, "Suit yourself." Pushing him back down.

. . . GIRL GETS AROUND

Zeke Chamas was giving her shit, talking like it was her fault some guy had been tailing her. Looking around now, no sign of anybody, just the two of them and the empty schoolyard. His Nova ss pulled up to her bumper. Zeke asking, "So, where's this guy?"

"Well, gone now."

"Can see you're buzzed." Zeke was pissed, getting the two calls back to back, this bitch with the mouth thinking she was being tailed. Then Sticky calling about catching some guy in the corn, turned out to be this bitch's bass player, ripping off Marty's field. Zeke told him to put the guy on ice, had to explain what he meant. Said he'd be out as soon as he took care of some business. Told Sticky not to do nothing till he got there.

Looking around now, he said, "Want to tell me what all that was, calling me from the gas station?" Zeke wondering if she had any part in her bass player ripping off their weed.

"Told you, some guy was tailing me. Had the look, you know, dark shades and a hat on. Behind me since I got off at Grandview."

"You panic, you draw attention. Next, you start making mistakes. The shit you been smoking's making you stupid. Come on, Frankie, you been doing this how long? Got to learn to chill."

Her look said, this from you? Drawing a breath, she said, "Anyway, I got back in the car, and the guy was gone. Maybe I gave him the shake, who knows?" She frowned at him.

Zeke told her to follow him over to Mitchell's Garage.

"Thought I was going to Euphoria's?"

"Enough with you doing the thinking, okay?"

"Fine. Mitchell's."

•

FOLLOWING HIM over to the garage meant she'd be seeing Bobby the mechanic, guessing he was scoring product from Zeke now, doing a little sideline. Maybe she'd get a chance to ask about that deal on tires, thinking again she should have returned one of Bobby's calls.

She followed Zeke in his jacked-up ride, dark-green Nova ss with the white stripes down the hood, the guy screeching his fat rubber as he took off. Rod Stewart puking from his Benzi Box, Rod selling out, asking was he sexy. She pictured Zeke hitting the discos on his own time, into Donna Summer singing about bad girls. Dancing with the two-inch heels under his shit-stompers, doing his disco moves to "Le Freak." Frankie grinning, wishing she had more hash.

Sticking in a cassette, the recording she'd made off

D.O.A.'s self-released *Disco Sucks* EP. D.O.A. drowning out Rod pounding from Zeke's subwoofers, the Nova ss with the twin tailpipes and fat slicks sputtering just ahead of her, Zeke with all the windows rolled down, all those decibels pouring out over the neighborhood. Frankie thinking, yeah, fucking guy telling her about not drawing any attention.

. . . ZEKE HEIL

ZEKE STOOD and waited on the sidewalk, still wondering what to do with the guy Tucker and Sticky caught in the corn. Frankie del Rey's bass player, the kid who worked at Falco's, sweeping the floor. All this shit just too close to home. All of it on his first day on the job.

Frankie walked from her Karmann Ghia, going to hand him the pink bag out front.

"You nuts? We do this shit inside. Jesus," Zeke said. "And next time park the fuck down the block, bring the bag in the back." Zeke glancing around.

"Fine."

Bobby stepped from the garage in the grease-monkey coveralls, name in cursive on his chest, pulling a rag from his back pocket, wiping at his hands, catching Zeke's frosty mood, but sticking out his hand, get their business off to a good start.

Looking at the hand, Zeke angled past him into the garage, Bobby looking at her like what's with him, saying, "How you doing, Frankie?"

"Doing alright, Bobby, you?"

Bobby shrugged, looking at the pink bag she was holding. "Guess it's business, huh?"

"Yeah, well . . ." Frankie said, following Bobby in, not sure why she never called him back, the guy not bad looking, filling out the coveralls in a nice way. Saying she hadn't seen him at the clubs, Bobby saying this place kept him pretty busy.

Zeke turned to them, saying to Bobby, "Need your office for a bit."

"Sure thing." Bobby didn't have one, but he pointed left of the service bays, guessing the break room would do.

Stepping over a pool of oil in the bay, Zeke went into the room, checking out the crappy table, sections of the *Sun* strewn across it, two metal chairs on either side. A counter with a filthy coffeemaker and an electric kettle. A jar of Sanka with no lid, another of Coffee-mate. Sugar and Sweet'N Low packets in a heap.

Frankie followed him in, Bobby stepping behind her, going to the table, straightening the paper.

"The fuck you doing?" Zeke asked him, throwing a thumb, meaning for him to leave.

First time she noticed Bobby's teeth were kind of buck, the guy smiling, looking awkward, his arms full of newspaper, saying, "Sure thing." He hesitated, looking out to the old Vauxhall on the second hoist, his apprentice working the lug wrench, taking the back wheels off. "Ought to help him put on the new drums."

"Still doing tires, Bobby?" Frankie said.

"It's a garage, right?" Bobby said, glancing at Zeke, remembering the state of her tires. "Got a couple on display out front, Michelin and Goodyear. I were you, I wouldn't let it go till winter." His arms full of newspaper, he hooked the door with his foot, Bobby started to close it on his way out.

"Hey, Bob . . ." Digging his keys from a pocket, Zeke tossed them, the keys bouncing off the name on Bobby's chest. Bobby juggling the paper and picking up the keys.

"How about giving my ride some fresh Valvoline," Zeke said. "Parked right out front. And while you're at it, rotate the tires."

"Sure thing." Looking at the Nova fob, Bobby shrugged, guessing this was a freebee, putting them in a pocket.

Zeke snapped his fingers, saying to Frankie, "Now, you give him the bag." To Bobby, "Dexies, like we talked about. I'll pick up my money on the way out."

Crumpling the paper under an arm, Bobby took the bag and unzipped it, checking inside, thinking of Marlon Brando talking the way he did in that movie, wanting to tell Zeke he should've had a consigliere give advice on his choice of gangster wheels; the Nova sticking out like a sore thumb, jacked up in the back with the fat tires, noisy header pipes and intake manifold. Bobby shutting the door.

"That was going to Euphoria's," Frankie said, looking around the room, pretty sure she smelled bologna. A smudged pinup calendar over the Mr. Coffee. Miss August showing her airbrushed titties, fingers laced behind her head, a look that said come and get it boys, the girl looking happy to be violated, a greasy thumbprint across her midriff.

"How about you let me worry about what's going where," Zeke said.

"Whatever."

Out in the garage, the sound of a power tool, Bobby going out and rolling Zeke's Nova inside the doors, raising her on the second hoist, getting to work, draining her oil and twisting off the filter, yelling who took his puller.

With Bobby busy, Zeke stepped to the door, putting his back to it, closing it and saying to Frankie, "A couple things we got to get straight here." Zeke knowing Marty was done with her after the shit she pulled in Falco's can.

"Yeah?"

"From here on, you go through me. So we're clear, I'm sick of your pissy attitude."

"Not the guy delivering flowers anymore, huh, Zeke?"

The slap sent her back against the coffeemaker, Zeke catching her in the mouth.

"Jesus Christ." Frankie putting a hand to her lip, glaring at him, not thinking, taking a swing.

Zeke catching her hand, made it look easy, not letting go, his grip crushing her fingers in his hand. Grinning, saying, "You had twice the tits and half the mouth, we'd get along fine . . ." Shoving her back against the counter.

She saw Bobby looking on, standing under the Nova, pretending he didn't see it, Frankie wishing he'd man up and cut this asshole's brake lines.

Reining in the temper, Zeke shook out the hand, silver ring catching the light, giving her a smile, thinking that didn't take long, saying, "Had that coming for the grief with the flowers."

Touching her lip, she leaned back against the counter, the filthy coffee carafe at her back, Frankie wanting to hurl it.

"Now, we get to business," Zeke said, knowing Bobby was

watching from under the Nova, Zeke setting an example. Frankie looking at him, nothing more to say, feeling the sting of the slap.

"Been having second thoughts about you playing in the barn." No way after Arnie Binz got caught ripping off their weed just ahead of the harvest. Still wondering if she knew about it. Marty letting a punk band in there, churning enough noise to draw any patrol cops going past the place.

"It's fine with Marty. Told me himself it makes things look natural." Frankie touched her lip.

"Yeah, see, that was back when Marty was thinking of getting in your pants. Man likes all that dinner-out business, candles on the table shit, putting on a show. Ask the chick back for a drink . . ."

Frankie looked along the counter, hoping for something sharp, saying, "Heard from Tucker, the locals've all been warned off."

"See, there you go again, telling me something," Zeke said, liking this.

Staring at him, she felt her fingernails digging into her palms. She'd have to call Marty back, try to reason and hope for the best. No reasoning with this guy.

"Other thing," Zeke said, "I'm changing the drops."

"And what's that mean?"

"Means no more running across the border like clock-work. Too easy to get tailed for real. From here on, I call and tell you when and where. Never the same thing twice."

"So, what, I'm like on standby?"

"Yeah, like that."

"You don't mind, think I'll call Marty," she said. "Want to hear it from him."

His eyes flared, then he let it go, saying, "Your next run's tonight. The barn, going to Euphoria's. Want it there at nine sharp, time they close."

"Can't tonight."

"Yeah, you can. Dropping a bag of dexies."

"One like you just gave Bobby."

"Yeah, just like that."

"I do it . . ." Her nails biting into the meat of her palms, "but first, I rehearse."

"This one time, but the bag's at Euphoria's at nine." Zeke shrugged, enjoying himself.

"Fine."

Opening the door, Zeke called to Bobby under the chassis, saying he'd be halfway done if he wasn't watching shit that had nothing to do with him.

Bobby was smearing oil around the filter's seal, setting it on and giving it a twist, wiping his hands on the rag. Thinking he'd like to drive his Volvo up behind this son of a bitch sometime, tap his ass end with his bumper, the gas tank hanging down under Zeke's rear bumper. Do it hard enough and watch his tin can burst into flames. One less asshole to worry about.

"And make sure it's the Valvoline," Zeke called. "None of that crap you smear in your hair."

Frankie walked from the room, stepping between the hoists, rolling her eyes so only Bobby could see.

"You okay?" he said.

"Yeah, fine."

"You want the tires, give me a call," Bobby said. "Let you have 'em at cost."

"Thanks, Bobby." She touched his arm and walked out to her Karmann Ghia, running her tongue over her swollen lip, thinking she'd like to even the score, find a way to pit one asshole against the other, Zeke versus Marty. Stand back and watch it happen.

. . . GOING DEEP

THE FOG had lifted by the time he showed up. Stepping from his Nova, parked behind Arnie Binz's Pinto Cruising Wagon at the shoulder of the townline, Zeke was thinking he should have worn his old boots. Flaring his nostrils, he was sure he smelled cow shit from somewhere. Jesus, how could anybody live out here? Driving along the back road, his paint pelted by gravel. No nightclubs, no broads, nothing to do but jerk off and smell cow shit. Hicks driving their pickups and wearing overalls.

Walking around back, he lifted the hatch. Reaching under the spare, he took out the Beretta, a model 81 with its serials filed off. A .32 auto with the plastic grip, fit in his pocket, with a big clip, a dozen rounds. Zeke liking it for its double-action lockwork, meaning you could fire with the hammer down, just a double pull on the trigger. *Bam*. Real fast. Set him back a few bucks, but this one was super clean. He didn't bring it for Arnie Binz, more like an equalizer if things went sideways between him and Tucker. If he used it, it would be just the one time, then he'd toss it off the

Ironworkers Bridge. The kind of thing that kept guys like him out of prison.

He considered the Wilson baseball bat under the battery cables, the Johnny Bench model, but instead took the leather-wrapped blackjack hidden under the carpet by the wheel well, liked the way it handled out back of Lubik's.

He walked the ditch to the edge of the corn, mud squishing under his boot soles, the two-inch heels caked in muck before he got to the fence, some getting on the leather tops. Scraping a sole against the post, Zeke saying, "Fuck me."

Waiting by the fence, he scraped the other sole on the rail. The one called Sticky was coming through the corn, snapping and swishing, parting the stalks, grunting as he pushed his way through. Zeke had no use for this half-wit Tucker hired to make the hash and watch the fields. Didn't have much use for Tucker either, nothing but big and sweaty, a guy Marty hired to run things out here. Zeke allowing that Tucker had a few more IQ points over this one coming through the corn, but it wasn't saying much.

Sticky slipped and grabbed hold of the fence rail, looking down at whatever tried to trip him. A three-day growth and dew on his face, breathing hard, the ball cap askew on his head, bandana around his neck, the guy smelling like cabbage. Looking at Zeke now, saying, "Hey ya, Zeke, how you doing, man?"

"Do better if you didn't keep me waiting."

"Sorry, started through the corn soon's I heard you coming down the road. Was Tuck had me call, you know, get your view of things, the best way to handle the situation."

"Yeah, so where's this situation?"

Motioning, Sticky turned and led the way, holding corn-stalks back like he was holding the door for Zeke.

Following the half-wit through the corn, Zeke bet he'd get them lost, tempted to just put one in back of his ball cap. Do everybody a favor. At the very least, kick a Frye boot up his scrawny ass. Zeke looking down, more muck caking on the leather.

"This way." Sticky pushed through the corn, coming to the edge of the field.

Tucker stood with his arms folded, looking at them, dropping his smoke and stamping it out, saying, "The fuck took you, professional driver like yourself?"

Arnie laid on the ground at his feet, with his hands and feet bound. A pair of socks tied end to end, shoved in his mouth like a gag.

"Think I sit around, waiting for you bozos to call, tell me you got a problem?"

"Yeah, come down here and show us how it's done, huh?"

Arnie craned his neck to look up, hard to see with his right eye nearly swollen shut, trying to keep the panic down in his gut, recognizing Zeke, the psycho who drove Marty Sayles to the club. Trying to make eye contact, Arnie seeing the blackjack in his hand. Knowing he was in for more of a beating. At least that.

"So, what's his story?" Zeke said, one hand palming the blackjack, smacking the business end into his other palm, feeling its heft.

Sticky saying, "Arnie here says he was out for a walk."

Arnie pushed his tongue at the socks, trying to roll over, wanting to talk, explain things to Zeke.

"That right?" Zeke put a boot on Arnie's back, pushing him down, saying to Tucker, "Get that out of his mouth." Pointing at the gag with the blackjack. "Disgusting."

Tucker gave him a look, this city boy put in charge, the one who did the driving, now coming out here and telling him what to do. Taking his time, he bent and pulled the socks from Arnie's mouth. Felt like stuffing them in Zeke's mouth, rip that club out of his hands and shove it up his ass.

Zeke took a stance like some golf pro, holding the blackjack down low, a nice two-handed grip, saying to Arnie, "Think I seen you around Falco's, I right?"

Arnie nodded, said his name, then, "Yeah, like I told these guys. Got my days mixed up, thought we had rehearsal, see, I'm the bass player, you know me. So I figured —"

Zeke pulled back with one hand and swung for the ribs, felt the thump, watching Arnie writhe, waiting through his groan, then saying, "Wanna try it again, Arnie, only tell it straight up this time? Only way it's gonna work, you with me."

Arnie nodded through the pain, felt like something was broken in his side, a stabbing when he breathed.

"So, let's start with an easy one . . ." Zeke tugged the knees of his pants, knelt down, wedging the blackjack under an arm, saying, "No way you did this alone. That fuck you work for, Falco, he in on it, right?"

"Just me. Like I said . . ."

Zeke glanced at Tucker.

"Somebody cut the tops the last day or so," Tucker said, "got every plant in this field. Different footprints."

"Only field that got hit?" Zeke said.

"Looks like, yeah," Tucker said.

"So, let me tell you about me," Zeke said to Arnie, getting up, smoothing his pant legs, taking that golf stance again, the two-handed grip, Frye boots proper distance apart, looking at Tucker, telling Sticky to back up a step. Then saying to Arnie, "You ripped off the wrong people, making me drive out here, that's strike one. Lying to me, that's two. Now I'm gonna ask one more time. And so you understand, it's a three-strike game."

"Zeke, right? Look, I get high, do it a lot, not something I'm proud of, but sometimes my days get mixed up, you know how it is? Came out here for band practice, thought it was later, you know, so I went for a walk up the road, fresh air, clearing my head. Stepped off the road to take a leak and stumbled on the pot, no mistaking it, so, guess I helped myself to a bit. Didn't know it was yours, man, honest."

Sticky saying there were two full bags stuffed between the rows back there.

Zeke looked to Tucker, saying, "Gag this fuck back up." Waiting for him to do it, swatting the club at corn cobs, busting some stalks. Sticky getting out of his way.

Tucker got up, giving Zeke some room, not liking the show he was putting on.

Zeke raised the club, Arnie trying to talk through the socks. Zeke swung and went to town, raining blows on him. Arnie screaming and moaning into the socks, twisting on the ground, his one eye wild.

"That's it," Tucker grabbed the blackjack from him and pressed the flat of his hand to Zeke's chest, easing him back.

Zeke shook himself, breathing hard, saying, "You never do that again."

Tucker flipped the blackjack to him.

Looking down at Arnie, then back at Tucker, Zeke said, "And put this fuck someplace." Dropping the blackjack back in his pocket.

"Someplace like where?" Tucker said, the shotgun leaning on a stalk Zeke hadn't busted.

"Figure it out, my man. I got other shit to do." Zeke started walking along the fallow field, back out to the road. Felt the adrenaline rushing through him. Needed to think this through.

Arnie was moaning into the gag, blood dripping from his nose.

"What about his car?" Sticky called.

"Said figure it out."

Tucker wanted to grab the shotgun and blow Zeke off his feet, this guy being careful where he stepped, not wanting muck on his fucking boots. Tucker looked at Sticky, saying, "Put him in the shed."

"How am I —"

Tucker reached the shotgun, saying, "How 'bout you figure it out. And make sure he's fucking tied tight, then lock the fucking door." Tucker said he'd take care of the car; there was an old tractor path up the road, nobody using it anymore, keep it out of sight. Going through Arnie's pockets, not finding the keys, he asked Arnie if they were in the car, Arnie barely nodding. Tucker walked out to the road, Zeke ahead of him, stamping his feet on the gravel road.

"What we gonna do with him?" Sticky called after him,

Tucker just walking away. Then Sticky went through Arnie's pockets, finding a wallet, but no cash in the fold. "The fuck were you thinking?" Sticky said to him, putting the wallet back and propping him up. "Think you can walk?"

Arnie just moaned through the pain.

"Shit." Sticky not sure how he'd get this guy to the shed at the back of the barn, hearing Zeke drive off. By the time he pulled the shoelace from Arnie's ankles, he heard Tucker start Arnie's car. He got Arnie up on his feet, but he was in no shape for walking, Sticky having to retie the ankles, then leaving him on the ground. He hurried through the corn, going for the wheelbarrow tipped over behind the barn, hoping the row between the stalks was wide enough to cart Arnie through.

. . . KILLER LOOKS

RITA SAT back on the bed, another shift at New2Me coming up, the used furniture and auction house, directing her lazy crew on the loading dock, skating around the owner's niece playing manager, half her age, didn't have a clue. Hence the vodka in her hand. Taking a sip, she watched Frankie put on the shirt, a men's extra large from the Mission Thrift Store, looping and tying the tails, leaving the sleeves hanging. Wiggling into her patched Levi's, she rolled the cuffs, making one bigger than the other.

Rita not getting the look, saying, "How come a man's shirt?"

"It's the look." Frankie shrugged. A fashion statement that said, I don't give a fuck about fashion.

"And it hurt you to put on a little makeup?"

"What do you call this?" Frankie blinked her eyes, heavy on the eyeliner, going for that Egyptian look.

"Don't mean putting it all in one place. I mean laying down a proper foundation."

"All those layers you put on, no offense, Rita, kind of old school."

"Careful, girl."

Frankie smiled, saying, "One good sneeze and you got avalanche of the face."

Rita sputtering, both of them laughing.

"You know what I mean, you got a pretty —" Noticing Frankie's swollen lip, Rita stopped, saying, "That son of a bitch Marty put a hand on you?"

"It was Zeke."

"The driver?"

"Yeah, bit of a slap. Just letting me know who he is."

"An asshole, plain as day."

"Language," Frankie said.

"Hell with that, ought to press charges."

"Against the dope dealers I work for?"

"You're making me old, girl. And how about putting on a bra?"

"What, and hide these?" Frankie smiled, trying to lighten the moment, grabbing her breasts, pressing out her chest.

That got Rita laughing again, saying, "You should take better care . . ." There she went, sounding like a parent again, waving her off, saying, "Those are going to end at your knees, you keep it up."

"Like that *Playboy* granny," Frankie said. "You seen her?"

"Yeah, I have, and the way you jump around, girl, won't be long, and it won't surprise me, not a bit."

The two of them laughing.

Rita sorry she got started, saying, "Those perverts at this barn, I mean, why tempt them?"

"Could wear flannel, and that guy Tucker'd see fishnet. Then there's Sticky . . ."

"Least you got your band there, right, Joey and . . ." Snapping her fingers.

"Arnie, right." Frankie thinking about him. Left three messages on his machine, letting him know the rehearsal got moved up, letting him know she had to make the run at nine. Not like him not to call back, Arnie forgetting about everything else, but always up for a practice.

Rita rose and went and freshened her drink, the vodka helping her cope with going to work, asking if Frankie had changed her mind, jiggling her glass.

"I'm good, thanks." Taking off the shirt, Frankie went to a drawer and slipped on a bra, hadn't put one on in a while. Put the shirt back on, did up the buttons, leaving the tails out, checking the mirror on back of the door. Wondering how Johnny saw her, this guy a little older, Frankie considering whether that should bother her.

Rita coming back in, saying. "Much better." A drink in one hand, a pink toy gun in the other, holding it out to her by the stubby barrel.

"What's this?"

"Protection."

"From what?"

"The creeps. Guys that go around slapping girls. Just aim for the eyes."

"You serious?"

"Pepper spray, burns like crazy."

"Could blind a guy, right?"

"The kind it might blind deserves it, that and a swift kick in the . . ." Rita sat on the edge of the bed, flicked her foot in the air, spilling some of her drink.

Taking it, the thing made out of cheap plastic, Frankie pictured shooting Zeke. Couldn't imagine this thing stopping him. Asking her aunt where she got it.

"Mail-ordered it. Saw it in *New Woman* or someplace, I don't know. Had this other thing called a Beaver, full-page ad," Rita said, "For guys won't take no for an answer."

"Afraid to ask, but: A *what*?"

"Beaver. See, the way it works, you insert it, right?"

"Insert, like a . . . you're kidding me . . . oh . . ." Frankie made a face.

"Yeah, joke if you want, but let's say a creep forces his way, you know . . . the Beaver springs and bites him on the . . ." Rita waving her fingers.

"Pecker."

"Was going to say weasel, but, yeah, right into the meat."

"Oh, jeez, oh, but why call it that? Beaver, on account of the teeth?"

"Yeah."

"Oh . . . ouch." Frankie making more of a face.

"Point is, once it bites, it's got to be surgically removed, won't let go, see, on account of the bite angle."

"Beaver won't let go." Frankie covered her mouth, laughing into her hand.

"Bonus is, you've got an instant arrest. Not much the perv can say. Pretty clever, really. With some guys it's the only way." Rita laughing, too.

"Tell me you don't have one?"

"Thought about it, but how often . . . never mind. But, look, Frankie, take that with you, keep it in your bag."

Frankie thinking why not, dropping the pink gun into

94

her handbag. "Always looking out for me, Auntie." She smiled, then reached her flop-hat from the closet shelf, putting it on, twisting the brim, cocking her hip.

Rita saying, "Go with the boots."

"Was thinking my high-tops, easier to jump around," Frankie said, guessing easier to get away, too, then remembering she wanted to call Marty again, try and smooth things out, try and keep the rehearsal space past tonight, maybe get him to back Zeke off, this guy making changes.

Rita got up, refilling her glass one more time and going to get ready for her shift.

Watching her go, Frankie checked herself in the mirror again, hating the feel of the bra, the wire digging into her ribcage. Dreaded making a second call to Marty. Deciding to wait till Rita went to New2Me, where she made ugly look good. Planned to take off the bra before she dialed the number.

"HEY YA, Marty." Frankie leaned against the kitchen wall, black Bakelite phone to her ear, fingers playing with the curled cord.

Silence, only the sound of his breathing on the line, Marty finally saying, "You again, huh?"

"Yeah, it's me."

"You alone?"

"Yeah, how about you?"

"See now, there you go again," Marty said, "thinking you can talk like that."

"Alright, I'm sorry, look, Marty, the thing at Falco's . . . guess I was a little high . . . guess you were, too . . . me, I was just reacting, you know . . . the bimbo coming at me."

"Not looking for your sorry, Frankie."

"You even know the girl's name?"

Snorting, Marty said, "What the fuck you want, Frankie?"

"Heard the girl needed stitches," Frankie reining it in, going for sincere, saying, "Wanted to see how she's doing."

"Yeah, well, when Sally came around, it was a toss-up

who she'd call first, cops or lawyer. Can thank me for talking sense to her."

"Yeah, well, thanks, but, hey, she came at me, right?" Frankie said, "And maybe if you and me set some ground rules in the first place, that shit never would've happened."

"Thing you don't get, Frankie, there was no you and me thing. What, we went to the movies, dinner a couple of times. So there's no ground rules."

"Yeah, okay, fine." Frankie thinking of the Beaver, pictured setting one on him, biting down and needing to be surgically removed. How's that for ground rules, asshole.

"So, guess you heard from Zeke," Marty said.

Frankie betting he was grinning on the other end of the line, enjoying himself now, saying, "Yeah, he's acting all man in charge. Telling me he's —"

"We don't talk this stuff on a phone, right?"

"Hey, you asked. And, like you'd open the door if I came knocking."

"Might be fun to see, Sal opening the door, you two going for round two, her not as high and seeing it coming."

"Sal, huh, she keeping house at your place now, huh?"

"All you got to know, girl, from here on, you go through Zeke. He lets you work, well, that's up to him." Marty ended the call.

Frankie looked at the receiver giving her dial tone. She threw it, sent the phone bouncing off the Kelvinator.

Beep, beep, beep.

Frankie kicking the phone, telling it, "Fuck off."

. . . GOING MEDIEVAL ON THAT BITCH

DUMB THING to do, call up Monk, meet him for a late lunch at the Only, under the neon seahorse. Scoring a chunk of black hash. Monk asking why she wasn't getting bhang free off Marty.

Frankie sliding into the booth at the back, saying, "Yeah, really got to ask?"

Monk putting the rest together. Nick, the owner, coming over and taking their order, Monk going for the oysters, Frankie saying she wanted seahorse, like on the sign out front, Nick rolling his eyes, heard that like a hundred times, putting her down for oysters, telling her it tasted pretty much the same.

Lunch didn't disappoint, Monk picking up the tab. When they got out of there, she kissed his cheek, Monk getting on his chopper, Frankie going to her Ghia, dropping some of the hash on the car lighter as Monk roared off. Careful she didn't burn her still-swollen lip, Frankie toked in the sweet smoke, needing a buzz to take off that edge. It wasn't as good as the bhang, but it wasn't bad. Then she shoved the stick in gear and drove south on Main, going through town, her Flying V and amp on the back seat. The sky was clouding over, meaning it would be dark early tonight. Hated driving to the barn alone, especially since she hadn't heard back from Arnie. Joey Thunder saying he was driving down solo in his mom's Country Squire. Tucker and Sticky creeped her out, the pair of them set to go off anytime, both always staring at her.

The Clash cassette ended as she got to the bottom end of town, Frankie popping the tape out of the player, rolling across town, leaning to the glove box and fingering through the cassettes, sticking in the bootleg she made of *Bullshot*, Link Wray blowing her mind. Fell in love with the king of rockabilly the first time she heard "Rumble." The guy was the granddaddy of the power chord. Rockabilly done right.

Tapping her foot, getting into "Snag," she bopped along, hoping the combination of Wray and the black hash would ease her nerves. Working out the riff in her head the way Link played it, singing along to "Just That Kind." Tapping her hands on the wheel.

Checking her rearview, half hoping to see Johnny's orange ride two cars back, the guy playing Serpico with the stupid sunglasses and beanie on. The Ghia sending up a cloud of back-road dust all the way along Zero Avenue, nothing but a farm road running straight along the U.S. border, two countries separated by a three-foot ditch and scraggly blackberry brambles. Farm fields swished by, most of it corn, some cattle grazing in an open field.

"Switchblade" thumped through the Pioneer speakers, Link Wray getting her where she lived. Zigging around a pothole, she hit a section of road that was like a washboard,

Frankie having to eject the tape, saved it from getting chewed up from all the shaking, happened twice before.

Then she was rolling up on the farmhouse, the one Marty Sayles picked up in some kind of foreclosure deal. The house wasn't much, the barn was worse, but the property stood isolated, the nearest neighbor about a half mile away on the Canadian side, and nobody across on the U.S. side, just about a mile of marsh, nice and isolated.

Instead of looking for the gate, her eyes went to the rearview, saying to herself, "Something wrong with you, girl, dealing with guys like this." Knocking the mirror with a slap, her knuckles smarted, thinking she had to quit running Marty's shit, simple as that. Didn't matter what it paid. Didn't matter about the rehearsal space either. She'd find someplace else, and she'd get the money for the EP, just have to do it another way. She'd been waiting for the phone to ring, hoping to hear about another Battle of the Bands, something the *Georgia Straight* hosted at the Commodore, the winner getting a recording session at Little Mountain Sound, with Bob Rock at the controls. Frankie thinking a girl could dream.

She'd been at the first Battle when D.O.A. got passed over, their fans throwing bottles, not accepting that shit. Frankie catching the band again at the Canada Day gig at Stanley Park, playing that one with the Subhumans, those guys cranking out "Fuck You" like nobody's business.

Cops on horseback swooped down on everybody because somebody forgot to get a permit. Frankie had stood by an equipment truck, laughing, watching Shithead run off into the trees in that Nazi helmet, an open beer in his hand, never spilling a drop.

Some church group ended up letting them have their own park permit a few blocks over. The Christians packing up their picnic and letting the punks kick it for a couple of hours. Everybody going home happy.

Driving right past the gate now, she jammed the brakes, her bald tires grinding, the Ghia coming to a stop in the middle of the three-way intersection. The engine cutting out.

Getting it started again, she backed up to the wooden gate, pulled closed. Not a porch light on, the house dark. Just the glow of a light coming from the barn.

No sign of Joey Thunder or Arnie. Quarter to seven, leaving them a short practice. Frankie hated getting there first, should have caught a ride with Joey. The farmhouse in the middle of nowhere. No street lights down here, nothing but shadows and the swish of corn in the breeze. The pink gun in the bottom of her bag.

She waited for Sticky to come out and open the gate, picking out the bootleg Furies tape, picking Side A and slipping it in the player for the drive back, her tunes as important to her as gas was to the Ghia. Recorded this one live on Labour Day two years back, the Furies playing the weekend with the Lewd and the Skulls, a Hellrazors bash out in Matsqui. Was a shit recording made on her Philips portable with the handheld mic, but to her it was a collector's item. Recording it right before the Furies split up. She took out the Ramones cassette, too, put it on the passenger seat, save her having to fish in the glove box on the way back. Copied the Ramones album off Arnie's vinyl, a better recording made on Rita's Sony Betamax, the album with "Beat on the Brat," one of her faves: a hundred and sixty beats a minute.

When she first got the Flying V, this was the album, Frankie working out the power chords, Johnny Ramone's lightning downstrokes. Simple but righteous. Loved the way Joey sang the old Chris Montez number, putting an edge on "Let's Dance." One Rita remembered from back in the day.

Giving a toot on the horn, she waited for the porch light to come on, Sticky finally coming out the screen door, a scrawny guy picking his teeth. In the light of her head-lamps, his jeans looking shiny from not being washed, flip flops and an attitude, his thumbs hooked in his belt loops. Frankie seeing the gun in his belt as he came to the gate, leaning on it. The guy taking his time. No wave hello, no smile, a real piece of work.

Rolling down her window, she said, "Hey, Sticky, how about opening up?" Frankie looking around, no headlights coming along the road.

Giving her a deadpan look, Sticky kept on sucking his teeth.

Even swinging on a stripper pole with old man fingers sticking bills into her G would beat putting up with this shit. Thinking about "five years past L.A." had her tapping her horn again.

Sticky jumped, bitching at her as he unlooped the rope that held the gate, pulling the gate back, letting her roll up the hard-packed drive. Grumbling, asking if she ever heard about the fucking word please.

Leaving the four-speed stick in first, she shut it off, pulling up the spongy handbrake between the buckets, telling him Arnie and Joey would be along anytime. Sticky shrugged and shut the gate anyway, looped the rope around the top.

Pulling her beat-up guitar case from behind the seat, she said, "Be a pet and get that?" Glancing at her amp, saying, "Please."

Sticky stood with thumbs in the belt loops, tongue working between his molars. Not making a move.

"Too heavy, I'll ask Tuck." She turned up the drive, knowing he'd get it. Going past the house, guitar in hand, handbag with the pink gun over her shoulder.

Sticky reached in behind the passenger side and grabbed the twenty-watt Alamo Futura Reverb by the handle, nearly put out his back, giving a grunt, leaving the car door hanging open, leaning to the side as he followed behind her.

Frankie smelled something like boiled socks wafting through the kitchen's screen door as she walked by, thinking laundry, but guessing it could be food. Looking back at him, saying, "Home cooking, Stick?"

Sticky saying it was cabbage soup, way his nanna did it. Made enough for the week, asked if she wanted a taste.

Frankie saying she was good, told him she just had some seahorse back in town, walking toward the light spilling from the barn, Frankie wishing Joey and Arnie would hurry the fuck up.

. . . BY THE SKIN OF THE TEETH

MAN, HE hated looking at the stack of receipts for the past month, the school notebook he used as a ledger open on the bar top. Johnny would be happy to turn it over to the woman who came in and did the books once a month — numbers not his thing. It didn't take a bookkeeper to point out he was barely scraping by. Selling Marty Sayles's pot gave him some breathing room. Johnny planning to hand Zeke half for the back rent, any more and him or Marty might ask questions, like where the money came from.

The knock at the front door had him looking up. Zeke Chamas standing in front of the closed sign, hand up like a shield to the glass, eyes peering in.

Speak of the devil.

Johnny didn't make a move, thinking what, these guys smell money? Then, taking his time, he stacked up the receipts, closing the ledger. Zeke knocked harder, looking pissed, calling, "Hey, you deaf in there, Falco?" Rattling the door handle.

Johnny shuffled to the door, seeing the guy's green

muscle car behind him at the curb. Flicking back the lock, Johnny stepped aside.

"Ain't got time for your bullshit, Falco." Zeke pushing his way through, scowling at him.

"Then maybe try calling first."

"Did call you." Zeke looked like he wanted to do something, saying, "Know why I'm here, right?"

"You want me to guess?"

"Hand me the fucking money, asshole." Snapping his fingers. Zeke stomped his foot, knocking dried mud from his boot. Two-inch riding heels giving him enough lift to make them nearly eye to eye, close to Johnny's six feet.

"Like I told you on the phone, I'm getting it."

"Yeah, so you got it?" Zeke stomping the other boot.

"Give you what I got so far. Get it while you sweep up." Johnny glanced at the floor, then pointed at the push broom leaning against the far wall.

"You want to try me, Falco, just say the word." Zeke snapped his fingers, the other hand hooking his belt loop.

Johnny went behind the bar. Opening the register, he reached in, counted out half what he owed, Zeke watching him put the rest back, shutting the register with a ding.

"What's stopping me from taking it all?" Zeke tugged back the jacket, showing the pistol butt, looking serious.

"Norton," Johnny said, slapping the money on the bar.

Zeke looked around, not seeing anybody. "Yeah, he hiding someplace?"

Reaching the shelf under the register, Johnny put the pistol on the bar, hand on it, the barrel pointing at Zeke. "Norton."

Zeke considered his chances of drawing his pistol, saying, "Man's not gonna like it, I come back light."

"Least you'll be coming back." Johnny looking serious, finally saying he'd need another week for the rest.

"Uh uhn, you got one more day."

"Then you come back tomorrow, but make it at night." Johnny keeping his hand on the Norton, saying, "And let's hope for the best."

"Better do more than hope, Falco." Zeke slowly reached for the bills and tucked them away, then with his eyes on Johnny's he said, "Let me ask where you were yesterday — say, early."

"Where you think?"

"How about the kid works for you?"

"Arnie? Have to go ask him."

"Yeah, and where do I find him?"

"Likely be here tomorrow night."

Grinning, Zeke said, "You two got a thing? You know, both of you into that fag music?"

"Not the first thing you got wrong today, huh, Zeke?"

His grin faded, Zeke looking at the Norton on the bar, then turning for the door, telling Johnny he'd be back tomorrow.

. . . CROTCH ROCK

Tucker liked looking at her, but didn't want her here. The music was always loud as hell, horrible shit to listen to; and now, the bass player lay trussed up in the shed out back. Zeke had called up, saying Frankie could play one last time, but still not saying what he wanted done with Arnie Binz. Tucker needing to focus on the harvest, set to start curing tomorrow, truckloads coming in from the other fields over the next couple of days. Hanging the plants from the clotheslines they'd string from the barn's rafters.

The RCMP had upped the regular patrols along the border since they busted that tunnel just a couple miles up the road. Three guys tunneled through the floor of a garage, breaking the concrete and digging their way all the way under Zero Avenue, running their meth across to the U.S. side. Till some nosey neighbor reported suspicious activity and noise one night, jotted down some license plates, all three of the guys with priors, two skipping on their parole. Gave the cops cause to come knocking, bringing along a search warrant. Charged all three with two counts of possession of a controlled substance along with possession of amphetamine precursors and paraphernalia. Nothing new about drug busts down along Zero Avenue, border-jumping practically a sport since back before the Volstead Act.

"Know this is it, huh? Last time," Tucker said when she walked into the barn. Coming over and standing a little close to her, a sour smell wafting off him, the same checked shirt he had on last time, a Molson's bottle in his paw.

"Miss me already, huh?"

Behind him stood some kind of rig that looked half constructed, an upright frame made of angle iron welded onto an old boat trailer, a welding cart and a red tool chest taking up the space the band would need. Frankie thinking redneck sculpture.

"Zeke said it was okay," she said, guessing Tucker already knew that.

"Zeke, that guy . . ." Tucker saying it like he might spit.

"What we got here?" Frankie said, standing the guitar case down, looking at the rig, middle of the rehearsal space.

Sticky came in and set the amp down, going to the cooler by the wall, fishing out a stubbie beer bottle, the opener hanging from a string on the barn wall.

"You want to play, you work around it," Tucker told her. Lengths of cut angle iron lying next to the rusted trailer. Tools and beer bottles and a couple of crushed Coke cans lay scattered around. The welding cart and tool bench next to it, a portable radio on top, aerial sticking up and out like a V.

"How're we supposed to do that? This thing's taking all the space."

"I look like I give a shit?" Tucker said, sounding irritated. "Is what it is, and you don't touch nothing."

A thump coming from out back. Tucker looking at Sticky, telling him to go take care of that. Sticky taking his beer, hurrying out the side door.

Frankie saying, "Look, Tuck, it's cool with Zeke, long as I make a run tonight. That's the deal."

Already heard it. Tucker knew about the run, another curve Zeke threw at him. Zeke calling in the afternoon and wanting another bag of dexies ready to go. Tucker sucked down the rest of his beer. A pot-growing operation with live music, just begging to be raided. Marty had put Tucker in charge of the place, planting the pot and keeping the farmers in line, leaning on them when he had to, making up the bhang, running the place like a distribution center, hiding all kinds of drugs in here, creating hidden compart-ments and false floors. Now the man was sticking too much powder up his nose, shoving Zeke up the ladder, in charge of the whole operation, the guy who didn't want to get muck on his boots, ones with the two-inch heels.

"Marty know about this?" Frankie said, trying a different tack, guessing what the rig was for. "A catapult, right?"

"None of your business." Grabbing it by the trailer tongue, he lifted it, biceps flexing, a couple pieces of angle iron dropping off. "Jesus fuck, you see what happens you show up?" Veins in his thick neck looking like they were set to pop. Tucker jerked the rig closer to the side door, giving the band some room.

"Sorry, Tuck, really." Frankie looking down the driveway again.

Setting the trailer to the side, he muttered something she didn't catch, picking up the angle iron that fell, tossing the pieces by the wall, wheeling the welding cart next to it. Scooping up the goggles, hanging them over a valve. Tossing his empty bottle to the far wall, he went across to the Igloo cooler, cracking another beer, drinking and wiping his mouth, looking like he might spit beer at her.

"So, it what I think it is?" Frankie pretending to take an interest.

"Why you want to know?"

"I don't know, just curious."

Tucker saying it was just an idea he had.

Frankie saying, "So, you're gonna shoot shit across, right?"

"Yeah, well, after that bust, guys with the tunnel . . ."

"Yeah, heard about that. Just up the road, right?"

Tucker pointed west, saying, "Why we got Mounties driving back and forth all the time now."

Frankie nodded.

Tucker saying, "Reason you're done tonight." Adding he wanted her to dial the volume down, too.

Wondering how to play punk with the amps turned down, Frankie heard another thump from somewhere out back. Curious about it.

Tucker went over to the workbench, burping up beer, switching on the radio, spinning the dial, finding a country signal coming from Bellingham, Ned Miller doing "From a Jack to a King." Tucker saying to her, nodding at the catapult, "This baby'll shoot two kilos at a time, maybe three, over as far as the trees." Tucker pointed to the grove out past the marsh on the U.S. side. The silhouette of the trees maybe three hundred yards off.

"Yeah?"

"Pssshuuut."

"Kinda like a giant slingshot," Frankie said, acting impressed, looking at the rig again, then out at the distant trees and nodding.

Freddy Fender coming on and singing about wasted days and wasted nights.

"Yeah, I can see it working," she said, "firing it at night, right?"

"Course at night." Surprised she seemed interested, seeing how it meant her job, no more muling dope across the Peace Arch. Marty's crew able to just shoot it across the border.

"So, you figured where it's going, I mean, when you shoot it?" she said. "Get Murphy's guys to pick up on the other side."

"Working all that out." He went and held the rubber sling, looked like a giant inner tube with a seat like a catcher's mitt in the middle, saying, "Control it by the tension on the rubber, see?" Pointing to a ratchet with a crank handle on the frame. A hook that the loop fit into. "I get it figured, and she'll drop in the same spot every time."

Frankie checked out the thick rubber, saying, "Think Marty's going to be impressed."

"Yeah?"

"Yeah, for sure." Looking some more at the contraption, the blackened angle iron around the welds, rusted trailer over flattened tires, Frankie picturing Tucker shooting bricks of pot across the border, landing them in the marsh on the U.S. side. Seeing the RCMP patrolling along, seeing packs of shit propelled across international space. Wondering if the cops had a ten-code for it. This farmhouse at the T intersection, in the middle of nothing. But still, Frankie thinking it wasn't any dumber than a tunnel.

"Think it's funny?" Tucker said, looking at her.

"No, no. Think it's cool, really. Not something Zeke'd come up with, that's for sure." Frankie getting how the big man felt about him.

"Zeke, that guy . . ."

"Yeah. Hear about Marty sending him by my place with flowers?"

That got him laughing, saying, "This after the thing with the crazy chick in the can, the punk joint?"

"Jeez, guess everybody knows, huh?" Frankie nodding, thought she heard another thump over the music, coming from out back.

Tucker smiling, thinking she wasn't so bad, turning the radio up some more. "Pay to see something like that, you clocking that chick, Marty with his . . ." Tucker forced a laugh, pissed on account of the thumping, Sticky supposed to be taking care of it. Watching Frankie checking out the rig now, looking at the swing arm on a swivel bracket attached to the cross member.

Glancing down the drive, she was wondering what the fuck was taking those guys, nearly full dark now. A little over an hour and she'd have to split to make the run to Euphoria's Top Floor.

"Two bricks at a time, huh?" she asked.

"Yeah, could be more. Like I said, it needs some more playing."

"Well, I'm impressed, Tuck. Think you sure got something here."

"Want to see it, I mean while we're waiting?"

"What, now?"

"Yeah, a little demo, you know. Just takes a minute."

"Yeah, sure, that'd be cool, thanks."

Lifting the trailer by the tongue, he wheeled it out the side door, another piece of angle iron falling off. The deflated tires made it hard to push, Tucker telling her he kept the pressure low on account the wheels kicked back when he fired it. "Got a hell of a thrust." His eyes wandering down her front.

"Cool." Fishing in her bag, she reached her pack of smokes next to the pink gun.

"Can't let you smoke in here, know that, right?" Pointing to the straw on the dirt floor.

"Right, forgot." She dropped the pack back in her bag, looking back down the driveway, thinking fucking musicians. The last song faded, and Eddie Rabbitt started singing the theme to some Clint Eastwood movie on the tinny radio.

Tucker set the tongue down outside, the wheels over two marks spray-painted on the dead ground. Just enough light spilling from the bulbs in the barn. The cedar hedge at the front of the property blocked most of the view.

Scanning around for a rock or something, he found one and hefted it for size, explaining, "Kinda big, so hard to know where it's dropping, but . . . why I got to have all that down when I start shooting bricks for real."

"Sure." Nodding, wondering if he really worked this out himself, this guy with the name of a family pet. Could be

Sticky had a hand in it. Sticky coming back in the opposite side door now, leaning on the far wall.

Setting wedges behind the wheels, Tucker took a length of looped rope hanging from the frame, lassoing one end of the swing arm, pulling the seat end down, slipping the loop around the hook under the seat. The other end of the rope was tied to the frame. Cranking the rubber tight, he attached it to the trigger, counted clicks as he ratcheted the handle, saying, "All set."

"Want me standing back?"

"Not gonna bite you." Tucker laughed, glanced inside at Stick at the far wall, didn't like the way he was looking, telling him to get him a beer, Sticky just standing there, kept looking at him.

Frankie saying she'd get it, going to the styro cooler next to Sticky. Tucker setting the rock in the catcher's mitt. She fished a bottle from the ice, smiling at Sticky, bringing it to Tucker. The guy not offering her one.

Knocking the cap off on the frame, he said, "Here goes," and hit the trigger. The arm swung up with a whoosh, the rock propelled into the air, making it over the cedars, dropping out on the road, Frankie watching, hearing the grinding of tires on gravel.

Somebody yelling, "Jesus Christ."

"Bit heavy," Tucker said, telling Sticky to get out there and see what the fuck was going on.

Keeping a straight face, Frankie recognized the voice, Sticky hustling down the driveway, hand on his gun. Headlights turned into the driveway, and Joey's station wagon pulled in, headlights washing the barn.

Tucker nearly took out her drummer with a rock. Frankie telling him again he had something here, watching Sticky out by the gate, letting Joey Thunder roll up the drive.

Wheeling the rig back inside, Tucker pushed it off to the side, offered her a sip of his beer, Frankie saying no thanks. Past the glare of headlights, she saw Joey open the rear gate of the wagon, packing half his drum kit on a dolly, rolling it into the barn, steadying it with his hand to keep the bass from rolling off, the rest of the kit still on the roof of the Country Squire. Joey coming in, saying, "Hell of a greeting. What the fuck was that?" The rock big enough it would have caved in the hood of his mom's Ford wagon.

Tucker shrugged, Frankie biting her teeth into her lip, saying nothing. Joey looking at the rig, straight out of *Popular Mechanics*, then at Tucker, saying, "That like a catapult or something, man?"

"You come to play, right?" Tucker folded his arms, attitude back on full. Charlie Rich singing about closed doors.

Joey Thunder looked at it, knowing what it was, thinking why not just walk the shit across the border, like at night, the way everybody else did it, only a ditch and a marsh in between.

Frankie was plugging a cord into the amp, Tucker explaining about wind and velocity to Joey, Frankie patching the cord to her fuzz pedal, then plugging the power cord into the extension cord running into the snake running out to the generator.

Tucker went out and fired it up.

"No shortage of surprises tonight," Joey said to her, going back out for the rest of his kit.

Frankie switched on the Alamo amp, setting the volume halfway, getting that creamy overdrive, twanging her strings, adjusting the tone, wondering what the fuck was taking Arnie. Turning the peg on her A string, getting it tuned, did the same with the D.

Tucker coming back in, telling her again to keep it down.

"Yeah, yeah." Frankie thinking any lower and the drums would drown her out. Looking to the drive, her heart jumped.

Jesus!

Johnny Falco was walking in with Joey, the two of them talking, Sticky pushing the other dolly behind them. Arnie's Musicmaster amp in Johnny's hand, the Thunderbird case slung over his shoulder. Frankie looking at Joey, Joey shrugging, saying, "Thought you knew."

"What the hell?" Tucker moved past her, arms held out, blocking the doors, saying, "Whoa, whoa."

Sticky left the dolly and went over to the cooler, thinking this should be good. Seeing what Tucker would do, Johnny Falco walking in here, the boss of the guy they had tied up in the shed.

...JOHNNY THUNDERBIRD

SETTING DOWN the amp, Johnny swung the gig case off his shoulder, unzipping it and lifting out the Thunderbird, reaching in the side pocket, taking a rag to it, the black body, white pick guard. Acting like he'd done it a hundred times, like he didn't notice everybody looking.

"Asked you what the hell?" Tucker said, voice getting loud, getting in Johnny's face.

"Here filling in," Johnny said it like it was obvious.

"Says who?"

"I asked him," Frankie said, covering for him. "Arnie's a no-show, came down with something, I guess, so I asked Johnny. Hard to play with no bass, right?" Frankie said, adjusting her guitar strap.

Tucker asking what happened to her regular guy.

Frankie saying, "Like I said, cold or something. Left him a couple messages, but haven't heard back. Know how these guys get, sometimes they show, sometimes not. Johnny just doing me a favor, filling in."

Tucker backed off, but didn't like it, the real bass player

out back in the shed, tied up, with Tucker's socks stuffed in his mouth.

Sticky walked back to the house, his Swanson in the oven, fried chicken with mashed and apple cobbler. He knew who Johnny was, leaving Tucker to sort it out. Could be they'd end up dealing with both him and Arnie Binz before the night was done.

The phone in the kitchen was ringing when he went through the screen door, Sticky grabbing the oven mitt first, taking his entree from the oven, setting in on the stove, then picking up the ringing phone. Zeke Chamas on the other end, asking what the fuck took him.

●

TUCKER WAS still eyeing Johnny, saying, "You even know how to play that?"

"Yeah, picked up a thing or two at the club. Ought to come down some time, check it out."

"Just fags in leather's what I heard."

"Hey, dress any way you want. We don't judge."

Frankie got between them, Johnny plugging the cord into the amp. Not bothered by Tucker, the guy looking like he was about to go off on him. Johnny slinging on the bass, heavier than he thought.

Tucker going around her, getting himself another beer.

Frankie stepped close, plugging in his power cord, adjusting the volume, saying, "What the fuck, Johnny?"

"Like I said, thought I'd sit in."

"You play, huh?"

"Everybody asking me that. Just four strings, right? How hard can it be?" Half the guys playing his club sounded like it was their first time.

"You hear from Arnie?"

Johnny said he saw him this morning, nothing since. Johnny went up to his room, checked his message machine, heard she was looking for Arnie, wanting to come out to the barn. Johnny wanting to have a look around, taking Arnie's bass and amp from his storeroom, leaving him a note.

Sticky came back from the house, the entree in hand, oven mitt holding the tray, fork in his other hand.

"Okay, let's do this," Frankie said to Joey, enough time to run through a few numbers.

"How about after?" Johnny said.

"After what?"

"Figure we could use a drink."

"You mean like you, me and Joey?"

"Was thinking just the string section." Johnny smiling at her.

"Got to make a drop first."

"You want, I'll tag along. Didn't drive the Scout or I could keep three cars back, follow you again."

"And scare the shit out of me some more."

Johnny plucked a few notes. Didn't know a fret from a riff.

Tucker and Sticky looked on from their usual spots by the wall, Sticky eating from the tray of Swanson, saying something to Tucker. The big man looking pissed at what he was hearing, drinking a beer, his three-day stubble mopping up what didn't make his mouth. His eyes stayed fixed on Johnny.

Frankie hated the unease, but she and Joey needed to run through a few tunes ahead of the gig, Johnny Falco faking some bass riffs, looking around the place.

Tucker saying at half past eight he was cutting the juice. Going to the styro, dipping his hand in for another beer, snapping the cap off on his belt buckle, sucking down a mouthful, keeping ahead of what was foaming from the bottle, saying something to Sticky. Sticky talking back, biting into a piece of chicken, thinking it should've gone longer in the oven.

Tucker slapped the Swanson tray out of his hand, Sticky looking like he might pull his Colt. Then turning, he kicked at the tray and walked out of there, back to the house.

Joey Thunder looked at Frankie, adjusting the snare, tapping his sticks, Johnny thumping the E string, fretting the third, plucking a G, alternating to open E. To him, it sounded like something.

Frankie shrugged at Joey — they could have gone with a cardboard cutout of Sid Vicious on bass, something Buck Cherry joked about after the Modernettes' bass player quit. Back before Mary-Jo came along, the girl playing bass like nobody's business.

Rifling the opening lick in E, Frankie took them into "Rumble." Johnny alternating between the two notes, bopping his head like he was getting into it. They limped through the number, Frankie plugging her mic into her second channel. Joey tapping it out, taking them into

"Fever," Johnny working the same notes, fingertips getting sore from fretting the fat strings.

Tucker went and got his own dinner, a can of Dinty Moore, didn't bother heating it, standing back at the wall, thinking about Zeke Chamas's call, the new boss man wanting them to take care of the guy in the shed, not being specific. Thinking he should call Marty up, hear it from the man, what he wanted done.

Frankie chased the song down with some "Jailhouse Rock."

Didn't sound any worse than the time she sat in with Rude Norton, a drunken fuck band, Dimwit and Wimpy Roy changing instruments, jamming out TV tunes, calling it "Tits on the Beach." Band members changing instruments, creating their own warm-up act, calling themselves a fuck band. Warming up the crowd for the Pointed Sticks that time, the gig at the Quadra, the leather crowd loving it. Frankie getting to know Nick Jones after the show, telling her how he got started with a band called Greased Pig, doing mostly Bowie covers. Second time she played in a fuck band, it was D.O.A. doing it, calling themselves Victorian Pork, her on guitar, Joey Shithead sitting behind the drum kit, guys from the Viletones and the Ugly getting on stage, taking turns on the instruments. Everybody too drunk to care.

Tucker tossed the empty tin at the Swanson tray, folded his arms and watched Johnny Falco playing bass like shit, the guy glancing around the way cops did. Sitting in for the guy they had trussed up out in the shed. Arnie Binz had been out in the shed since early morning, waiting for Zeke to figure things out.

Tucker not liking the way the day had gone. Frankie had taken an interest in the catapult, Tucker thinking she was seeing him in a new light, then Johnny Falco showed up.

Frankie played one of her own, Joey Thunder backing the vocals, "I'm a runaway," getting that raw sound.

Eight thirty on the nose, Tucker signaled it was time to wrap up. Saying again the farmers went to bed soon as the sun sank. Telling Sticky to fetch the pink bag, filled with dexies.

Slipping the Thunderbird in its case, Johnny said to Tucker, "So, what did you think, my man?"

"Think you're no Geddy Lee."

"Yeah, that guy can play. Funny, figured you more the Kenny Rogers type."

"Something else you got wrong." Tucker tipped back his beer, going out the side door, killing the generator.

Johnny went to the cooler, looked at Sticky, saying, "May I?"

Sticky just turned and walked back to the house, didn't want to push the dollies heaped with gear back out to the wagon. Johnny helped himself to a Golden, went to the amp and pulled the cord, zipping up the bass.

Packing his kit on the dollies, using the bungee cords, Joey was happy to get out of there tonight, not liking the way Johnny Falco was swatting at the hive, standing there drinking their beer.

Johnny offered the bottle to Frankie, saying, "Wasn't so bad, huh?" Looking at the catapult.

"Heard worse," she said, but not sure when. Sipping some beer and handing him the bottle.

"Yeah, well, Gibsons practically play themselves." Taking another sip, he looked at Tucker coming back in.

Casing her guitar, Frankie wound a cord, Joey wheeling the dolly out to his Country Squire.

Tucker stepped over, grabbing Johnny's beer and tossing it over at the Swanson tray, saying that was it, closing time, then to Frankie, "Like how you did 'Jailhouse Rock.'" Handing her his own beer.

"Thanks, Tuck. Didn't know you were into it." Forcing down a sip, handing it back.

"Lot you don't know. But the King, can't go far wrong there. Am I right?"

"Yeah, true."

Sticky came back holding a second tin tray, warmed in the old Radarange, the label on the tray warning about putting it in the microwave. The pink bag in his other hand, bringing it to Frankie. *Gee Your Hair Smells Terrific* down the side.

Tucker told him to go refill the cooler.

"I'm eating," Sticky said, forking Swanson into his mouth, shaking his head and going to the wall.

Tucker turned to her, saying, "Hang around if you want. Got lots more beer."

"Got to make the run for Zeke, remember?" Looking at Johnny, saying, "You want a lift back?"

"Yeah, thanks." Shouldering the bass, Johnny picked up the amp, walked by Tucker, thanking him for his hostility.

Tucker snagged his sleeve, stopping him, saying, "You don't come back, understand?"

"Came down to do me a favor," Frankie said.

"Think you heard me." Tucker let go of the sleeve.

Johnny walked out, Frankie picking up the pink bag and grabbing the amp.

Feeling the urge to pee, telling herself it would have to wait. No way she was going in that house, the can probably looked worse than the one at Falco's. Helping Joey Thunder load up the wagon, she was happy to get in the car and get out of there.

. . . THE SWEET SPOT

HAULING THE catapult to the center of the straw floor, Tucker set down the trailer tongue. Needed to get some spot welding done, add on the braces, get it right. Tomorrow he'd test for distance, send Sticky out to mark the spots, Tucker wanting to fire bricks as far as that grove of trees. A spot Murphy's guys could use as a nighttime pickup point. "Jailhouse Rock" stuck in his head, the way Frankie sang it.

The girl had taken an interest. Seemed it was real, maybe there could be something there. This chick who used to go with Marty Sayles, good enough for the boss.

Going to the house, Sticky came back and dropped more beer in the Igloo cooler, the ice all melted now. Looking at Tucker, watching him set the arc lamp in position, swatting at flies buzzing around his head.

"What about what Zeke said?"

"Fetch me one," Tucker said, without looking at him, positioning the light over the frame.

"Something wrong with your feet?" Sticky done with being the lackey.

Fast for a big man, Tucker was across the floor, bouncing

Sticky off the barn boards. Sticky windmilling his arms, tripping on an empty bottle, down he went, landing on the Swanson tray and Dinty Moore tin. Tucker went to swing his boot, Sticky's hand on the pistol caused him to stop.

"Gonna draw on me now, Sticky?"

"Not going off on me like that. No more." Sticky's hand stayed on the grip, telling himself he'd do it, getting his feet under him and slowly rising.

"Stop pissing me off, and you stop getting hit." Tucker backing off.

"I mean it, Tuck, no more." Brushing straw and bits of food from his pants and shirt, Sticky straightened his cap. Guessing if he ever drew, he'd have to pull the trigger. No turning back. Sure he could do it, just not something he wanted to explain to Zeke Chamas. The way Zeke had laid that beating on Arnie Binz with the blackjack, the sound of it hitting flesh, doing it like he enjoyed it. Arnie Binz hogtied out in the shed all day, waiting.

"Just 'cause you say it, doesn't mean it's so." Tucker looked at him, betting he didn't have the stones. Getting his own beer, he turned back to his toolbox, shoving box wrenches around the top tray, finding a file, saying, "That fuck walking in here, strapping on the other guy's guitar . . . and that asshole Zeke, calling up and telling you to get it done. Not saying what the hell he meant, pussy footing around."

"Didn't ask me, said for us to decide."

"Ask me, the two of them were in on it."

"Who?"

"Falco and the one in the shed," Tucker said. "Why he came here, looking for his buddy."

"Crossed my mind, too." Sticky swept his foot at the tray, tin and spilled food, sweeping it to the corner. Had to get a trash bag from the house, didn't want to attract the rats.

"Truly fucked is what it is," Tucker said, looking at the catapult. "Letting them in here, sound of their shit music carrying for miles, and with all we got going on . . ." The way Tucker saw it, Marty was into the blow too much, and Zeke was like a mad dog off its leash.

"So, what are we gonna do?"

Tucker looked at him.

Sticky not liking the look, had enough of getting hit. Telling himself he'd pull this time, the Colt with seven rounds. Started carrying it for show, kept it under his jacket going into places like Oil Can Harry's, back before it closed, saved him from a couple of beatings. Could have used it that time at Orestes, place with the belly dancers. Sticky getting roughed up by the bouncer for putting his hand on one of the girls wiggling her butt, Sticky giving her a fat tip, thought the two of them had an understanding, turned out he was wrong. Another time, two assholes tried to roll him in the john of the Commodore, followed him in, Sticky letting them see the Colt, both of them backing off. Sticky pretty sure if he had to take it farther, he could do it, pull on a man and shoot. Wanted people to understand that about him.

Tucker swept his boot at the straw, getting it away from the torch, telling Sticky to get some dummy loads ready for the morning.

"Like what?"

"Rocks, something weighs the same as a couple of keys,

more or less. Got to get the velocity and distance right. Gonna be doing it for real."

Sticky just looked at him, this guy firing up his welding torch, straw all over the dirt floor. Likely to burn the place to the ground.

Tucker looked at him, setting a brace in place, saying, "Just gonna stand there sucking on beer, leave all the work to me?"

"How about the guy in the shed? We putting off dealing with him?"

"You took the call, go ahead and deal with it."

Sticky thinking about what to do.

Tucker setting braces back in place, thinking about Zeke Chamas coming here with his little club, doing his cute golf swings. Beating the man more than he needed to. Putting on a show, careful about getting mud on his boots, leaving his mess and walking off.

Going back out the other door, Tucker fired up the generator again. Sticky was gone when he came back in. Tucker thinking he could go out back and put the fear of God into Arnie Binz, then turn him loose, take a chance he wouldn't go to the cops. Or he could keep him locked in the cellar of the farmhouse till they cured the weed and got it all out of here. Tucker played back the way Johnny Falco just showed up, the way he was looking around, checking out the catapult, helping himself to a beer. Likely looking for signs of Arnie Binz.

Tucker tightened the band, using the box wrench. Firing up the torch, he pulled on the welding beanie, slipped on the goggles and turned the torch valves. Donning the gloves, he held a brace to the frame and tack welded it in place, then put one on the opposite side. When he finished up, he turned off the torch and flipped up the visor. Grabbing another Molson from the cooler, he watched Sticky come back, setting down an armload of pumpkins.

"Fuck, I told you rocks," Tucker said.

"You know it's dark, right, man? These were growing near the road, easy to spot. Got about the right weight."

"Yeah, but the size is wrong. And how about the color?"

"Making them easy to see, you know, where they land."

"Easy to see's the point. Somebody over there sees flying pumpkins, won't take much to put it together, what we're doing." Tucker went to the cooler, taking another bottle from the ice water, tossing it to Sticky.

Reaching the opener dangling from the wall, Sticky popped off the cap.

"I been running it through my mind," Tucker said, nodding to the shed. "Gonna let you handle it."

"What?"

"You take care of Binz. Put the fear of God in the man. That or put a bullet in him, your choice. Way you been carrying that pistol like a hard-on, I can see you're itching to do it."

"Saying we shoot the guy?"

Tucker just looked at him and shrugged.

"This is you just trying to pass the buck."

"Not me that needs the bragging rights." Tucker pushed the torch stand over to the wall.

Sticky watched him do it.

"Nobody talks shit to me. Won't to you either, not after

something like that. Guy goes back after you walk him out and made him dig a hole, him feeling sure he's about to get shot. Scare the shit right out of the man."

"So, dig a hole, like a grave."

"Yeah, right, only make him do the digging, get him believing it."

"Shoot him or no?"

"Well, that part's up to you. You don't, then you just got to make it real, like I'm saying. Do it right, and you probably don't need to shoot him. You want, put one past his ear. Up to you how you do it."

Sticky rolled it around. Just walk the guy out. Jab the pistol at his back. Make him dig the hole, get him believing he's going down there, his life flashing by. Fire a round past his ear. Tell him to take off and don't look back.

"Ground's soft out there, past the corn, right?" Tucker said.

"Guess so."

"He gets done digging, steps out the hole, you get him to turn around, just walk away while he's expecting it. Time he figures it out, he's just happy to be alive."

"Still could change his mind, open his mouth to the cops."

"Okay, so you shoot him."

"Yeah, but somebody could hear."

"Locals know better than to say jack shit, right?" Tucker looking at him. "But, the point is, the shooting part's optional. Like I'm telling you, you scare him enough, make it real, then you don't need to."

"Yeah." Sticky seeing it. Just walk him out in the field,

untie his hands and make him dig as best he could, being all beat up. Just have to make him believe it. Never get easier than that. Could spin a story like that any way he wanted, get all kinds of respect, guys buying him drinks, hook up with women he didn't have to pay for. People calling him Lenny Lowe, nobody calling him Sticky anymore.

"Course, if you're worried about him talking, and worried about the sound," Tucker said, "then you press the barrel into him, right here," Tucker pointing at his own belly, "and shoot. It muffles the sound."

"Now you're saying shoot him."

"Like I said, Sticky, leaving it up to you." Tucker having fun playing him, turning back to his rig. Tucker thinking of Zeke Chamas — wouldn't mind shooting that fuck himself. Then there was Johnny Falco. Him, too.

. . . CATCH THE WIND

"Okay, so he fires this thing," Johnny calling it Tucker's chucker, saying, "but how's he know where it's going?" Looking at her behind the wheel.

Flipping on the FM, Frankie shrugged, driving her Ghia back along Zero Avenue, letting the radio play till they got past the washboard part of the road. CFMI transmitting pop tunes off the top of Mount Seymour. Only other signal out here was scratchy news from CKO, that or country.

Guitar cases and amps in back, another pink bag filled with dexies, Frankie going to drop it off at Euphoria's, just off Commercial. Joey Thunder driving just ahead, the wood-grain wrapping the Country Squire. Roof racks on top. Frankie eating his dust, backing off, feeling that shimmy start from the front end.

"Like I told you, girl, I figured the hell out of that puppy," Frankie mimicking Tucker, saying, "Ain't that so, Sticky?"

Johnny laughing. "Sticky, that guy . . ."

"Yeah, they walk among us." Eyes on the road, she popped in the live tape she made of the Furies, knowing he liked them. The band kicking off with "What Do You Want Me to Be."

A car came the opposite way, its high beams flashing at them, raising more dust as it rolled past. A cop car, looked like an LTD, patrolling the border. She could barely make out Joey's taillights now, way up ahead.

"Guy thinks he can nail the same spot every time, doesn't matter about wind or rain." Johnny checking out her cassettes in the glove box, most of them bootleg recordings, saying, "Marty know about it?"

"Not yet."

"Picture him flinging Marty's pot into orbit, see it landing in that swamp," Johnny said.

"It's not such a bad idea," she said, "he gets his distance right, does it at night."

"Come on. Got to do better than the rock he fired over the hedge, nearly took out Joey's wagon."

The two of them laughing about it, Frankie saying that was Tucker just showing off.

Then they were talking about the gig tomorrow night, Frankie jazzed about it, but worried about Arnie going off the radar, not showing up at rehearsal. Johnny assuring her he'd show up, just the guy's nature, seeing she was worried. Changing the subject, saying again he wished he'd been around to catch the Furies.

Frankie telling him about the show at PUMPS, then getting invited to the Matsqui bash where she recorded the tape, shortly before the band split up. The Lewd and the Skulls on the same bill. Told him how the bikers finally ran off the Lewd for not playing long enough, the Skulls scared into replaying their set list for like two days. The bands getting paid in booze and coke, all they could handle. Up on the stage, getting drunk and rude, pissing on the crowd and passing out on the stage. Still, there was more chaos offstage than anything the bands could dream up onstage. A hell of a party.

"So, how about that drink?"

"Alright, but at my place, and first, I got to pull over," she said, slowing and easing the wheel, feeling the tires grip the soft shoulder.

"Was thinking more my place." Johnny looking out the rear window, making sure they weren't being pulled over by the patrol cop.

"Sorry, got to pee." She pushed in the clutch, put the stick in first and shut it off. Joey's taillights were gone now. "No way I was going back there, Tucker looking set to go off on you." She flipped down the visor, took a couple of tissues from a Kleenex pack, smiled at him and stepped out. The grass standing tall and wet with dew past the ditch, Frankie nearly losing her footing, slipping down the ditch.

Walking through the grass till she was out of his sight line, she tugged down her jeans and crouched. The ground soft under her sneakers, crickets chirping all around, wet grass tickling her. Could hear the Furies doing "Sister Ray." Johnny with his arm hanging out the window, tapping his hand on the door panel.

Getting back in, she said, "Not a word, okay?"

Johnny showing his hands.

Turning the key, she worked the clutch, giving it some

gas, the night settling in. Frankie looking at him, saying, "Still want that drink?"

"Nothing scares me," he said. "Just want to know, you got indoor plumbing at your place?"

She was laughing, hitting a pothole, her shocks not up for the task, the chassis bottoming out, the tape getting caught in the player. Popping the cassette, saying, "Hate when that happens." Eyes on the road, she turned the take-up reel with a fingernail, taking up the tape slack, looping it around the cassette. She reached over and dropped it in the glove box, switched on the dome light, fumbling for the Ramones tape.

"Here let me." Johnny picking a random tape, pushing it in the player.

"Red Rubber Ball" coming through the speakers.

Not what she expected, Frankie switching off the dome light, looking at him, saying, "Know it?"

"The Diodes, you kidding me?" Telling her he met them back east when they started out, just a few instruments in some shitty basement dive at OCA, along with a bathtub full of ice and beer. Caught them again at a place called the Crash 'n' Burn. Good times in Toronto.

Frankie saying it was one of her favorites.

Stealing a glance at her, Johnny said yeah, "Tired of Waking Up Tired" was one of his. Telling her about the time he caught them at the Colonial, playing downstairs, drowning out Long John Baldry playing upstairs. The band refusing to turn it down, leading to the bouncers pulling the plug, leading to a riot spilling out onto Yonge Street. Johnny ended up in a paddy wagon with everybody else, all of them released the next morning. Saw the band again at Larry's

Hideaway, nobody arrested that night. Said he'd been trying to get them to come out west.

She loved the stories. Johnny telling her about catching the Last Pogo at the Horseshoe, put on by the Garys, another near-riot: the Scenics, the Secrets, the Mods and more on the bill. Just ahead of him moving out west, hitch-hiking his way across Canada. This guy older by a dozen years, into his old-school punk, loved bands like the Dolls, Velvet Underground and the Stooges, but open to the new sound, giving bands a chance at Falco's, putting up his own money to do it.

After she made the drop at Euphoria's, she walked back to the car, saw him watching her, Frankie guessing a drink would lead to two, two leading to bed — see where it went from there. It had been a long time coming, some-thing passing between them when he started sliding OVs across the bar, Frankie trying to pay him, the two of them talking, looking at each other, Johnny not making a move on account of the thing she had with Marty. Things looking different now.

. . . KILL FOR A GIG

FRANKIE WAS telling Johnny how it felt getting up on that stage, the butterflies in her stomach, just nothing like it. "Beats anything . . . you ask me." She was thinking *except sex*, looking at him, blue eyes kinda like the guy who sold her the car.

Johnny nodded, saying he got that.

The two of them on either end of Rita's leather sofa, Frankie having looked in the fridge for oj, finding none, pouring straight vodka, offering him ice.

Frankie telling him about finding some old 78s in Rita's cellar, back when she lived in the house in New West, before her uncle passed. Frankie teaching herself to play rockabilly, sitting on her bed every night and every weekend, getting it down while her girlfriends were out partying. Fingerpicking, learning slide, getting that lightning fretwork, adapting it to the punk sound.

Having Johnny over had her setting aside worries about Arnie, still no word from him.

Johnny asking about her set list.

Frankie running it down, knowing she'd have to stretch

a couple out, play some twice. Not enough for two full sets. They'd try a couple of original tunes they put together.

Johnny telling her about the posters being printed up, this guy Gregg who worked for his uncle's construction company, in the print shop. Gregg sneaking in after hours and running them for the local bands, did it real cheap, too. Calling his sideline Second Job Press. Johnny hired some kid after school, the kid running around tacking and gluing them all over the Eastside, at two cents a piece.

Frankie saying she was sorry about the Dishrags having to cancel.

"Don't look so sorry to me," he said, nudging her.

"Just a little." Smiling, telling him about the show at the Japanese Hall, the Dishrags opening for the Furies, back when they were starting out, saying, "Chicks were like fifteen then, but the sound was tight, you know?" Saw them again at the Lotus Garden, got to know Jade Blade a bit, sat in with them at the Laundromat, again at the SUB Ballroom, that one with Female Hands. On the bill at the Windmill on Granville.

"Heard about that one." Johnny saying he knew the owner of the Windmill, asking if she got paid, not something the guy was known for.

"Yeah, well, Stain kinda took care of it." Going to the Windmill, banging on the door with his fist, demanding extra from the guy for his trouble, coming back with her cash.

Grinning, Johnny knowing the big man's nature, thanking her again for the Waves filling in, Frankie saying she should be thanking him.

"Not exactly the Mab."

"Not yet, maybe," she said, "but you keep on booking bands like Middle Finger . . ."

"Guys doing their *yabba dabba do*s."

"The one they were playing . . ."

"Yeah, when you clocked the chick in the can."

Frankie making a face.

"People still talking about it," Johnny said, leaning close.

"You clean it up?"

"Naw, had Arnie do it. Back to normal, the can looking like it always docs."

"Not gonna let me live it down, huh?"

"Uh uhn. Likely pack the place just on that, the crowd coming to check you out."

"But not Marty or the blonde."

"Naw, wouldn't count on them too much." His hand going to the back of her neck, touching her hair. Setting his drink on the table.

Letting him do it, Frankie told him about adding a punk version of "Gloria," that oldie by Them, Van Morrison singing the hell out of it. The Waves version not as nice and easy.

Johnny asking if she ever did anything nice and easy.

"Wouldn't work with my me-versus-them attitude." She smiled, leaning a little closer, saying, "I mean, why go Anne Murray, you know, when you can go Patti Smith, right?"

"Like 'Snowbird' versus 'Pissing in a River.'"

"You got it."

He kissed her then, Frankie kissing back, the two of them on her aunt's sofa. Talking about touring down the coast, playing the Mab, Washington Hall and the Barn, all of that could wait. Frankie reaching for the lamp behind the sofa and pulling the cord.

•

AFTER, THE two of them were on the sofa, her head on his chest, Johnny with his shirt off, asking about the Waves' EP, Frankie telling him about getting demos out to Perryscope, hoping to sell copies through Quintessence. She sat up, tying the shirt, pouring a couple more shots, telling him about this promoter down in Long Beach, young guy named Swinson, friend of a friend. Met him backstage at the Dead Kennedys show at the Bird, place in Seattle. Partying with the warm-up band called the Blackouts.

Johnny watched her unfold some tinfoil, breaking off a piece and spearing it on a safety pin, Johnny fishing for his lighter, putting flame under it. Waiting till the hash glowed, he blew it out and leaned over her cupped hands, drawing the smoke off the pin. Hadn't toked up like that since that time in Ocho Rios, smoking spliffs the size of Cuban cigars, damned things wrapped in newspaper, this Jamaican guy named Emmett driving him around in a van, twenty bucks a day, the two of them drinking Red Stripe, Emmett showing Johnny how to vacation. High the whole week he was down there, could hardly remember the red-eye flight coming home. At the time he was saying never again.

"Hash's pretty good, right?" Telling him she copped it off Monk. Reaching her guitar from its stand, she played one she'd been working on, calling it "No Fun City," the guitar unplugged. Then she strummed the chords to an Iggy song, Johnny joining in on the words he could remember, the line about just being out of school.

A little more hash, a little more vodka, Frankie saying why not come down the coast with them.

"Know I can't sing."

"Can't play bass either, but that didn't stop you."

"Ouch." Johnny saying he had the club, Frankie saying she didn't have all the money yet, but wasn't letting that stop her.

"Got this idea, a way to make the money . . ." he said, wanting to tell her about robbing Marty Sayles.

Hearing the elevator from down the hall, she told him to hang on, took his hand and led him to her room. Wasn't sure when Rita's shift ended tonight, didn't want her walking in and finding them half naked on her sofa.

Closing her bedroom door, she switched on the bedside lamp, Johnny taking in her room. Frankie dropped his shirt and her bra, untied the loop of her own shirt and dropped it, saying, "So, what's this idea?"

"It can wait." Looking at her, Johnny pulled her to the bed, forgetting about robbing Marty Sayles.

. . . DOWN THE BARREL

THE ROWS between the stalks seemed to narrow in the dark. Arnie walked ahead, a shovel in his hands, the handle getting caught on a stalk. He pulled it loose and turned his head enough to see Sticky behind him, pointing the pistol, Arnie saying, "Don't need to do this, man."

Shoving the barrel at his back, Sticky told him to shut up and walk, shining the flashlight ahead of Arnie. Screwing up his courage. Tired of hearing the guy pleading. Told him to be glad he didn't have Tuck's socks balled in his mouth now. Forcing Arnie to walk between the rows, fifty yards into the corn. Sticky switched the pistol to his other hand, psyching himself to make this real, wiping his wet palm on his jeans.

Making it to the end of the row, Arnie stopped at the open field, nearly the same spot where they caught him. Sticky told him to start digging, pointing to a spot, told him how wide and how deep.

"Come on, Sticky . . ." Arnie still hurting from the beating, stabbing pain in his side, Arnie sure he had a concussion, a knot on the back of his head, dried blood crusted in his hair. Hardly had any water all day, and nothing to eat.

"Told you to stop fucking whining. Time for that's done. Now dig." Pointing with the pistol, Sticky told him again to do it, didn't matter how much it hurt.

Shaking his head, Arnie tossed the shovel down, saying, "No way, not digging my own grave."

"Fuck, I got to do it, I put this barrel to your knee, blow off the knee cap so you don't run. Gonna feel like nothing you racked up so far. Now do it."

"Going to shoot me anyway." Arnie crying, watching Sticky wiping his hands on his pants.

"Two ways to do this — the quick, then there's wishing it was." A voice inside telling Sticky there was only one way he was leaving this field as Lenny Lowe, burying Sticky in the hole right along with Arnie Binz. Pointing the Colt, he gritted his teeth, hissing, "Dig."

Bending for the shovel, Arnie stuck the blade in the ground, felt like somebody was spearing at his ribs. Shoving his foot down, he started to dig, driving the shovel into the soft earth, working through the hurt and tossing the earth, telling himself he had to do something, wait for his chance. He wasn't just going to let it happen.

Sticky kept the pistol on him, considered just chasing him off — his choice, Tucker had said. Arnie would be too scared to say a word about it, tell people he got mugged or something. In a week they'd have the pot cured and gone, and it wouldn't matter either way. Sticky switched off the flashlight, enough moonlight to keep watch.

Arnie stopped to catch his breath, swiping a sleeve at the

tears, saying, "A bag of pot, it's not something you get killed for, man."

"You fucked with the wrong guys, all there is. Now shut up and dig."

Sticky watched him, wanting this over. Seeing himself going back and facing Tucker, the fucker laughing, saying he knew he didn't have the stones, mocking him for taking the easy way out, letting Arnie go. Telling him to call Zeke and explain it. Switching hands on the pistol, wiping at his jeans again. Thinking he could use a whiskey. Told Arnie to keep going.

Arnie put his foot on the shovel, struck an old root or something, having to chip the blade around to work it free. He kept chopping the blade at it, having to stop again, saying, "Look, man, what am I gonna do, run to the cops and say I was ripping off your pot? I'm already on probation."

Sticky ignored him.

Striking at the root, Arnie worked till the sweat rolled from under his arms, his hands shaking. He stepped from the hole, saying, "Fuck it."

"Blow off your knee, swear I'll do it."

"Look, wait, we fill the hole in, then you fire a round in the air, and I'm gone. You go back and tell them it's done. Not like they're gonna dig it up and check."

"You don't know shit about it."

"Know one thing, you do it you got to live with yourself. Gonna wake up screaming."

Sticky clamped his teeth, hissing like he was letting off steam. Both hands on the grip, aiming at Arnie's knee, making him believe it.

Picking up the shovel again, Arnie stepped back in the hole and jabbed at the root, working it loose, feeling it come free. Scooping it onto the blade, he bent his knees and looked up past Sticky, saw his chance, saying, "Figures it'd take two of you."

Now or never.

Sticky turned his head, and Arnie flung the root hard at him, coming out of the hole, winding the handle of the shovel. Forgetting the pain.

Getting struck by the root, Sticky fired a wild shot. Knocked into the stalks, he kept to his feet. Arnie swatted with the shovel, knocking away the pistol. Sticky throwing up his arms, warding off the blows. Arnie swinging and hitting, laying a beating on him.

Sticky fell, everything spinning. A blow across his back put him flat. Rolling out of the way, he tried to get up.

Raising the shovel, Arnie swung like he was splitting wood, knocking him down again.

Feeling the pistol under him, his hand grabbed for it, Sticky twisting as Arnie swung. Firing up. The bullet went in below the collar bone, going out Arnie's back. He spun, losing the shovel, tottering to keep on his feet.

Sticky pushed himself up, the ringing in his head, the blood running past his eye. Lifting the pistol, he didn't think about it now.

Arnie lurched at him, and Sticky pulled the trigger.

Arnie flopped backwards.

Dropping to his knees, Sticky tried to breathe, feeling the blood trickling down his face. Right then, he wanted to go back to the barn and shoot Tucker, too.

He tried, but couldn't get himself to stand, sitting there three feet from Arnie splayed out. When he could stand, he threw up. He tucked his pistol in his belt, standing over the body, finding the flashlight, switching it on. Arnie's shirt was soaked, blood staining the ground, his eyes like a doll's. Sticky shone the light at the shallow grave. Then he heard movement coming through the cornstalks.

●

STARTED RUNNING through the corn when he heard the second shot, figured Sticky fucked it up, Tucker shielded his eyes against the flashlight beam. Sticky telling him to turn that thing off.

"What the fuck . . ." Tucker looked down at Arnie's body.

"It got done."

Didn't think he had the stones. Tucker stepped to the hole.

"Thing is, you gonna do it, Sticky, you make the other guy dig the hole first, then shoot him so he falls right in. Now you got to dig and drag him to it."

"Name's Lenny Lowe." Sticky bent for the shovel and tossed it at Tucker's feet, saying, "You dig it."

"You in no condition, huh, Sticky?" Tucker looked at the blood on his face, the look in his eyes, saying, "You with the gun, him with the shovel, nearly got the better of you."

"Told you, it's Lenny now." Sticky stood, ready this time.

Served him right for leaving the shotgun behind, Tucker stared at him a moment, then reached for the shovel.

Sticky put a hand on a cornstalk, Tucker putting his back into it, tossing dirt from the hole.

Should dig it deep enough for two. Tucker planning to call a guy he knew in Abbotsford who ran a chop shop. Have to get Arnie's Pinto off the tractor trail and make it disappear.

Sticky squatted down, fighting the spins.

"Guy decked you pretty good, huh? You with the gun."

"What the fuck you bring, Tuck?" Sticky kept his eyes on him, thinking if Tucker stepped out of the hole, he'd shoot him. Nothing hard about it.

Tucker saw it in his eyes and kept digging, there'd be another time. When it was deep enough, Tucker dragged Arnie by the ankles, flopping him into the hole.

Shovelful at a time, he filled it in. Tucker stamped his feet across the top, kicking some loose soil, making it look natural. Not another word between them, Tucker guiding Sticky by the arm, helping him between the rows, back to the house. Sticky kept a hand on the pistol butt, knowing Tucker wouldn't let it pass. He planned to wedge a chair under his doorknob tonight, and every night after. He'd clean and oil the nickel-plate, nobody needing to tell him to keep it close and loaded from here on.

. . . LEFT OF CENTER

"So, WHAT's this idea, you were starting to say . . ." she said.

Johnny propped up the pillow and leaned back, saying, "Going to rob Marty Sayles."

She just looked at him.

"You and me."

She sat up. "Come on." The blanket dropped down. "What, like play Bonnie and Clyde? Know how that ended, right?"

"Not going to be like that."

"Like, just walk up and say stick 'em up, asshole? Biggest dealer on the Eastside. Guy who keeps Zeke Chamas on a leash, and that guy just dying to shoot somebody."

"The way we do it, they don't know it's being done."

"Stop saying we."

"Then I do it alone."

"Who's watching too much *Five*-o now?"

"The man's got pot fields all over the Lower Mainland. With just the two morons down at the farm keeping watch."

"Ones with the guns."

"They won't know it's being done."

Laying her head back on the cushion, she looked at him. Could be the hash and vodka talking, Johnny taking an idea for a walk, Frankie saying, "Okay, so let's hear the rest of this plan."

"They're set to harvest, have to do it all at one time, curing it in the barn. We put eyes on the place and wait till it's cured, then pick the right time. Go in at night and drag bags of it through the corn out back, have a truck waiting on the townline."

Folding her arms behind her head, she played back the way he just walked into the barn with Joey Thunder, Arnie's bass in his hand, sure of himself. "That what you were doing, coming down to the barn, playing bass and planning a rip-off?"

"Yeah, that and a chance to play with the Waves."

"Man, it sounds . . . I don't know . . ."

"Could be a kick."

"More like desperate," she said. "And what about Arnie, you get him mixed up in this?"

"No."

She reached for the bottle, took off the cap and took a sip, passing it to him. "Okay, so, robbing Marty, I get that . . . the guy's an asshole who's got it coming; and Zeke, well, that's another story, but still . . . there's just you and me."

"Sounding more Anne Murray. 'Snowbird' instead of 'Pissing in a River.'"

She play-slapped his arm, the two of them lying there, Johnny setting the bottle on his stomach.

"Full of surprises, I'll give you that." Resting her head on his chest, thinking they needed coffee, not vodka. Things would look different, Johnny seeing clear in the morning.

"You want me to go, case your aunt comes home?"

"No, stay." Frankie saying her aunt was cool. She'd just come home and crash after her shift at New2Me, a night of moving furniture around.

"People bidding on used stuff, huh?" Johnny trying to picture it, old furniture with stains and mold.

"Place has an auction every couple of weeks, one of those guys talking a mile a minute. Throwing around words like vintage and one-of-a-kind. Rest of the time they tag up what didn't sell at auction. Rita sets the floor, making ugly look good. They hang a sign out front: open to the public, and you wouldn't believe it. Chairs, tables, rugs, old paintings, knick-knacks, anything." Pointing around the room, Frankie said, "Where most of this stuff's from."

"Yeah, well, this looks nice." He glanced at the chair, the dresser, gilt-framed mirror over top, Johnny seeing the two of them in the reflection, thinking of the crap he'd been dragging through his own life, always wanting to leave it behind.

"Really want to talk about what my aunt does?"

"Guess we covered it." Johnny set the bottle on the nightstand next to him, hand reaching across her for the lamp, asking if she wanted it on or off.

"Surprise me."

He kissed her, tasting vodka, Frankie's arms going around the back of his neck, and they were back into it. The two of them under the blanket. Taking it slow the third time around.

. . . HAIR OF THE DOG

HE WOKE first, light spilling between the partly drawn curtains, sounds of somebody out in the kitchen, the clink of dishes being washed, guessing Aunt Rita was home. Johnny hoping for the aroma of coffee.

Frankie opened her eyes and smiled at him, giving him a kiss, happy he was there. Stretching her arms over her head, the blanket falling away. "Pretty incredible, right?"

"Yeah." Looking at her.

"Meant last night."

"That too."

"Going to tell me it gets better with age, something like that?"

"Had to go there, huh?" Rolling on his side, he reached for the vodka, uncapped it and decided it was a bad idea. Bunching his pillow, he propped himself up. "You want?"

Frankie shook her head, hearing Rita in the kitchen, saying, "You ever try it with yogurt?"

"Vodka, you kidding?"

"Breakfast of champions."

"Don't even like it with fruit on the bottom."

"How about eggs, toast, something like that?"

"You got coffee, and I'm good to go." Johnny not sure if he was ready to meet the aunt, guessing she might be close to his age.

•

Rita had put on a pot of coffee and gone for a shower, Johnny hearing the spray from down the hall. Frankie on the kitchen side of the counter, putting in two slices and popping down the toaster. Sipping his coffee black, he swiveled on the stool. The hangover fog wasn't too bad, the coffee taking care of it. A stack of underground magazines, papers and fanzines on the counter: *Georgia Straight*, *Melody Maker*, *Iconocast*, *Flipside* and *Creem*. Some student paper called *Ubyssey*. Johnny leafed through an old issue of *Surfin' Bird*, skimming an article about the Chromosomes' break-up, a hot band who'd never recorded a note, the drummer jailed on drug charges. He told her about catching them back east, too, playing some private party, the guitar player diving in the pool, his electric guitar still plugged in. Somebody quick enough to yank the cord.

"Not the craziest thing I've heard," she said, looking at him.

"You mean the thing with Marty?"

"Really going to do it, what you said?" Frankie keeping her voice low.

"Been building it in my mind, yeah."

"Was hoping it was the booze talking." Standing across from him, buttering the toast, putting two more slices into the toaster, leaning her head to the doorway so she could hear the shower down the hall.

Johnny watching her, saying, "Got to find a spot on the other side of Zero Avenue, past that marsh. Put eyes on the farm. Check out the coming and going. Way I see it, they'll have crews bringing loads of it to the barn."

"And me?"

"Just make the runs for now, do like Zeke says. Keep a low profile."

She picked up the phone and dialed Arnie's number, frowned when his recording came on, and hung up. The toast popped up and she scraped on more butter, set the slices on a plate.

"Arnie?"

"Yeah." Then she said, "Can't believe he's gonna miss the gig." Trying to lighten the mood, she told about Buck Cherry, the Modernettes' bass player quitting, Buck wanting to set a cardboard cutout of Sid Vicious on stage, Buck usually high enough to do it.

Grinning, Johnny trying not to show his own worry, Arnie sometimes showing up late for work at the club but never missing a whole night. Johnny had left Stain the keys last night, let him and Monk run things. The last night for Middle Finger, the band taking their sound down the coast.

Frankie took a bite of toast, thinking she'd give it till noon, then call up this guy called Wimpy, ask him to sit in.

The knock at the apartment door had her jumping. A sharp rap. The two of them looking at each other, Frankie looking at the clock on the stove, hoping it was Arnie. Setting down the plate, she went to the door, didn't want

whoever it was knocking like that again. Putting an eye to
the peephole, she turned to Johnny, keeping her voice low,
saying, "Shit, it's Zeke."

. . . BURNS LIKE A BITCH

WAITING, PRETTY sure he heard voices inside. Set to knock again, Zeke heard the lock turn, the door pulled back.

Johnny Falco standing there. Eight o'clock in the morning. Zeke looking surprised, putting it together, his mouth going into a smile, hiding he was pissed off about it, saying, "You two, huh?"

"What do you want, Zeke?"

"Funny, didn't see your ride outside. The thing the color of fruit."

"They call it Omaha orange, Zeke. Funny, you saying something about another man's ride. Driving around all jacked up in the back."

"Call that a real man's ride."

"You got flowers, a message, something you want me to pass along?"

"Lot to say for a guy still owes the rent. Which I want, and I mean today. Now, you gonna step aside? Or you want, I can do it for you."

Frankie came to the door, bread knife in her hand,

tugging Johnny's sleeve, getting between them, saying, "What's up, Zeke?"

"What's this?" Zeke looking at the knife, butter on it, putting up his hands.

"Making my toast go cold. Ask you again, what's up?"

"Called, but just got your machine. Didn't figure you'd have company."

"That's my business, right?"

"Told you things are changing. So how about you ask me in, offer me a cup and I tell you what I want?"

Tugging Johnny out of the way, she let Zeke in, closing the door.

Going to the island, Zeke sat in Johnny's chair, pushing his mug aside. "Milk and three sugars." Zeke glanced around the place, taking it in, saying it looked real nice, then looking at Johnny, saying, "Something funny?"

"Naw, drink it any way you want," Johnny said, catching the bulge under Zeke's jacket.

Taking a piece of toast, Zeke bit into it, asking if she had jam. Frankie setting the knife down, getting out the Smucker's jar, pouring and sliding a mug his way, getting the sugar bowl. Opening the fridge for a carton of milk, sniffing it, she shrugged and put it in front of him.

Stirring a spoon around the mug, Zeke took his time, saying, "So, you two, huh? Ain't that nice." Pouring, he watched the milk curdling in his cup. Taking a taste, spooning in more sugar.

Frankie wondering what Johnny would do if he knew Zeke had slapped her at Mitchell's garage.

"Need you today," Zeke said, ignoring Johnny next to him, Johnny looking like he wanted to tip him off the stool.

"Yeah, about that, Zeke, this new way of doing things, don't think it's going to work for me. Have to pass."

"How you mean pass?"

"Means I quit."

Johnny looked at her, wondering how that was keeping a low profile.

"Think you just walk out, just like that?" Zeke said, spreading jam on his toast.

"You dope dealers getting two weeks' notice these days, Zeke?" Johnny said.

"Say another word . . ." Zeke turned on the stool, looking at him, the jacket pulled back enough to show the pistol butt.

"Sorry if it leaves you short," Frankie said. "You need somebody, maybe go ask Marty's bimbo, the one down on her knees."

"Yeah, you sure you want me saying that to Marty?"

"Say what you want."

Zeke looked from her to him, pointing a finger at Johnny, saying, "Not a fucking word out —"

Grabbing the finger, Johnny bent it back, the hand Zeke needed to draw with, giving it a twist. Johnny stood him up, got his arm up behind his back, pushing the arm like a lever, steering him for the door. Zeke cursing, trying to resist.

"What the heck's going on?" Rita came from the bathroom at the end of the hall, slinging the sash of her housecoat, towel around her head, puffy slippers on her feet, pink gun in her hand.

Johnny got the door and shoved Zeke out into the hall, shutting it, throwing the lock, saying to Rita, "Fellow was just leaving."

"He deliver more flowers?" She smiled at Johnny, guessing who he was, dropping the mace gun in a pocket.

Johnny said his name, then "Guess you'd be Rita."

"Yeah, the one who pays the bills, one who needs her sleep." Rita reaching past him, sliding on the chain. Hearing the elevator door ping open, then close down the hall. Turning, she looked at her niece, then back at Johnny, guessing the girl got herself a new rehearsal space.

"Sorry, Rita," Frankie said, "Guy just showed up like that . . . told him I was done."

"Well, that's something, the first smart thing I've heard." Nobody needing to tell her Johnny had spent the night, not sure how she felt about it, going past him and sitting on the stool Zeke had sat in, shoving his mug away. "Any coffee left?"

"I'll make more," Frankie said, going to the kitchen side, scraping more butter on toast, setting it on the plate, pouring out Zeke's mug, tossing out his toast, putting the plate in the sink, setting about making another pot.

"Like how you handled that," Rita said to Johnny, taking a slice of toast. "That guy sure had it coming."

He sat next to her, helped himself to a slice.

"Ought to see the animals I got to deal with, place I work," Rita said.

"That what the pink gun's for?"

"Guys generally don't like a woman telling them what to do."

"So you pull it on them?" Johnny smiled, liking her.

"I do what I have to."

Frankie asked if Rita wanted something else, getting her a mug, waiting for the coffee to drip.

Rita said yeah, the usual, and Frankie reached the tub of yogurt, then the bottle of vodka from the counter, setting both in front of her, getting her aunt a bowl and spoon.

Johnny watched her spooning Danone and pouring vodka over it, raised a brow, sipped his coffee.

"Most important meal of the day," Rita said, looking at the near-empty bottle, saying to Johnny, "She tell you about me, huh?"

"Yeah, a little, and about the place you work, how you make ugly stuff look good."

Rita smiled, nodding at his coffee, saying, "Top you up?"

"Wouldn't mind a splash, thanks." Johnny held out his mug, let her pour in a shot, saying, "Was thinking about doing my place if I stick around, you know, redecorate a bit. I do, I could use some help with it. Not really sure what I want."

"A lot of that going around," Rita said, looking at Frankie. Finishing the yogurt, she sipped her coffee, taking the mug and heading down the hall, saying it was nice to meet him, telling Frankie she had to be at work by two.

Frankie said they'd keep it down, looking at Johnny, hearing her aunt's door close, saying, "You hear her come in this morning?"

"Think so, yeah." Johnny saying, "I like her."

"Yeah, she makes a good impression."

Johnny drinking his coffee, thinking he'd keep the Norton with him from here on, start looking over his shoulder.

. . . BLOWBACK

"MAN'S GOT to go," Zeke said, standing at Marty's door. Nice big place up at the top of the Properties with a hell of a view, could see the Lions Gate below and all the way out to Mount Baker on a clear day. The laurels at the street hid the long driveway and three-car garage off to the side of the house. Nothing like this on the Downtown Eastside, where Zeke lived.

"Johnny Falco over at Frankie's, huh?" Marty said, standing, holding the door, smiling and sniffling.

"Yeah, looked like he'd been there all night. Just showed up at the barn, too." Zeke bending for Marty's paper, handing it to him, guessing by the glassy eyes the boss was high again. Zeke wiping his feet on the mat like he was expecting to come in.

"What do you mean he just showed up?"

"Heard it from Sticky, said Falco came and sat in with her band, Frankie's."

"And where the fuck were you?" Marty making no move to let him in, Zeke just standing on the welcome mat, just like when he played chauffeur, driving the man around, sitting behind the wheel of the Toronado, waiting, playing with the fucking radio knobs.

"Was taking care of things in town, like you wanted, dealing with Suzy and getting business lined up with Murphy."

"Taking care means taking care. Got to have your eyes everywhere. Know what's going on."

"Yeah, I know, I'm on it."

"And this fucker Falco, he still owe me rent?"

"Taking care of that, too. Already got half. Leaning on him for the rest."

"So lean harder."

"Have the rest of it today."

"You ask where he got it, coming up with it all of a sudden?"

Zeke saying, "Club's been picking up, I guess." Then seeing the blonde move behind Marty, couldn't think of her name.

"And this guy you caught in the corn?"

"Took care of it. Guy won't be talking." Didn't tell him it was Frankie del Rey's bass player.

"Far as the broad goes . . ."

"Frankie?"

"Yeah, she's done. I want her out."

"Already taken care of, fired her ass this morning."

"At least that." Marty stuck his paper under his arm and swung the door shut.

Zeke standing there feeling dumb, facing the closed door, hearing Marty talking to the blonde inside. Turning, he aimed to drop back down to Zero Avenue, make sure the harvest was running smooth. Tucker and Sticky having a way of fucking things up. This had to go right. No way he was going back to driving Marty around, picking up his fucking cleaning and delivering flowers to jilted chicks, taking the man's shit.

Walking down the drive to the Nova, he got in and fired her up, the rumble of the DynoMax pipes. He grabbed the wheel, his finger hurting, Falco grabbing it like that. Backing out, Zeke pictured catching Falco coming out of the club one night, the guy parking that orange shitbox out in the alley. Take him for a ride in the country and put a couple rounds in him and plant him out there with his buddy, nothing but miles of nothing, the guy twisting his finger like that. Doing it to impress Frankie.

. . . SHITHEAD

"Could be you're on the rebound," Rita said, dressed casual in jeans and a sweatshirt, her bare feet on the tiles, toenails painted pink. She considered the Absolut in the freezer, but it was getting close to her shift. Top of that, she only had about five hours' sleep. Two truckloads packed with an estate sale coming to the warehouse later today. Rita having to sort through it, decide what went straight to auction or to charity, what went in the display cases, what she'd put out on the floor, fill the showroom, Rita looking at another long night.

"Johnny's different," Frankie said, putting the last dish on the drying rack, draping the dish towel on top. Picking up the phone, she dialed Arnie's number again, then hung up, getting nothing but his machine. Reaching the open jar of Smucker's, the spoon sticking out, she took a mouthful.

Rita saying, "That's what bread's for."

"Less calories this way." Frankie saying, "You liked him, huh?"

"He's kinda cute."

"Not going to say he's older?"

"Let you worry about that. Main thing, you're done working with these people. No going back this time . . ."

"I'm done, promise."

Rita stopped from giving the "you're a smart girl, you can do whatever you want" speech, hated when she started sounding like a parent. Having made enough mistakes in her own lifetime. Raised this girl since Frankie was six — Frankie's mother killed in a car wreck. Rita and Frankie more like girlfriends. And Frankie wasn't a kid anymore.

"Should have seen him, Johnny, the way he showed up at the barn, sitting in with Joey and me. Just looking out for me."

"And then you brought him here."

"Yeah, well, one thing led to another . . ." Frankie gave a shrug, saying, "Sounds trashy, huh?"

"Was thinking spontaneous."

The two of them grinning, Frankie dipping the spoon in the Smucker's jar, Rita checking the clock on the stove, saying she had to go, then snapped her fingers, remembered something and reached above the phone, taking a sticky note from the wall. "Nearly forgot . . ." Handing it to her. "Shithead called."

"Marty?"

"This one was slurring his words. Called after you left yesterday, said he wanted you to call back. Hope I got the number right . . . all the noise in the background."

Frankie jumped for the phone, unlooping the cord, dialing the number. Getting no answer, saying, "Shit. Tell me again."

"Language." .

"Sorry."

"Sounded like a party going on. Was hard to hear. Just said for you to call, sure he said . . . well, that was the name he said. Something about coming back from Regina for the night. Opening for the Crash."

"The Clash?"

"And wanted you to call."

Frankie dialed again, putting it together, Shithead flew back from Regina, interrupting the band's tour to open for the Clash, the gig at the PNE Fairgrounds, not wanting to miss the chance. Last time she ran into him at the Buddha, he was talking about putting together another tour down the coast, hitting the Showbox in Seattle, the Revenge in Portland, the Mab in Frisco. Told her he'd talk to Chuck and Randy, set it up and get back to her. Said he wanted Waves of Nausea along. Talking about getting a big bus, doing it with the Subhumans, maybe the Dils and the Dishrags. He said he'd call when they got back from Regina. Wanted her to come to their gig at the Sub Ballroom, on the bill with Female Hands.

"People really call him that, huh?"

"Yeah, even his mom." Frankie dialed again, not getting through, saying, "Shit."

"Language."

"Sorry."

... MAN'S GOT TO GO

ZEKE TURNED off Zero Avenue, pulled into the drive, gravel crunching under the tires. The wooden gate was closed. A loop of twine holding it in place. A *No Trespassing* sign, the kind you got at any hardware.

Redneck security.

He tapped the horn. Waited, then tapped a little longer, thinking, Jesus Christ. Finally, leaning on the horn.

The side screen door opened, Sticky poked his head out, coming out with his jeans undone, a pair of work boots in his hand, waving for Zeke to stop fucking honking. Socked feet on the gravel, Sticky walked like he was on hot coals, doing himself up, hopping on one foot, shoving the other into a boot, asking, "Can't a man take a shit?"

Zeke laughing at him, drumming his fingers on the wheel, engine idling, betting this half-wit got his left and right boots mixed up.

A quarter million in pot down here, Marty Sayles putting Tucker and Sticky in charge of things.

Sticky unlooped the rope from the top of the gate,

swinging it back. Zeke inched the car in, tapping the horn again, loved the way Sticky jumped.

Jesus Christ.

Rolling the Nova past him, Zeke reached the Colt Super under his seat, the trigger getting stuck on a spring, Zeke easing it loose, afraid of it going off.

Sticky re-closed the gate, saying, "I supposed to know you were coming?"

"Day I got to make an appointment with you, Stick, day I shoot myself." Putting a boot out the door, the two-inch heel squishing in the muck.

Jesus Christ.

Took half an hour to clean them yesterday, Zeke sitting in his Barcalounger, in front of the Zenith, working in the dubbin, buffing the soft leather with a rag, took him all the way through a *Five*-o episode to get them looking right. Zeke loving when Jack Lord said, "Book 'em, Danno."

Looking at Sticky, seeing the pistol stuck in his pants, Zeke said, "So, what've you got there, Sticky? Take that in with you when take a dump, huh? Shootin' the shit."

Saying he didn't go by Sticky anymore. "Name's Lenny Lowe." Sticky cleared it, quick and easy, careful not to point it at Zeke, saying, "Colt Commander. Seven in the clip. Just blued her."

"Yeah, nice and shiny. Good for shooting cans off a fence, huh?" Zeke guessing that was like a sport down here. Showing his own Colt, nickel-plated, the .38 Super with the ivory grips, not worried about pointing it at Sticky.

"What the fuck?" Tucker stepped from the barn, wiping his hands on a rag, flinging it down. Careful where he stepped, the drive slick from last night's rain. "You clowns playing with your pistols, how about you don't do it down at the road, and what's with the fuckin' honking?"

"You and me need to get things straight, Tuck," Zeke said, putting the pistol away, walking toward him.

"Yeah, how's that?" Tucker said, his shotgun leaning by the barn door.

"The way you're talking, sounds like you didn't get word." Zeke walking closer, thinking if he made a move for the shotgun, he'd put a bullet in him. "About Marty putting me in charge."

"You ask me, the way you're stepping, careful about getting mud on your boots, you're looking more like a fruit than a boss."

"You want to make the call, hear it from the man himself, see what's what?"

"I make a call like that, maybe I tell him how his new boy's down here honking his horn, flashing his gun and begging for the law to stop by."

Zeke looked around, shrugged like he didn't see anybody.

"Two patrols by this morning, fucking chopper flying over couple days ago. Guess you didn't hear about that tunnel, huh?"

"Yeah, I heard." Looking from one to the other, not liking Sticky standing beside him, Zeke feeling flanked. "Next time, I don't want no gate in my face." He fished out his keys and tossed them, Sticky catching them.

"Pull her in, Sticky," Zeke said.

Tossing the keys back, Sticky said, "Don't do valet parking, and told you it's Lenny now."

"That so — Lenny, huh?" Dropping them back in his pocket, Zeke snapped the Colt out, pointing it, stepping so he could see Tucker at the same time. Zeke saying, "Take the gun out with your left hand and drop it on the fucking ground."

"Just blued her." Sticky doing it slow, taking it out and setting it down, stepping away.

Zeke tossed the keys again, Sticky catching them.

"Don't make me tell you again."

Sticky turned and walked to the Nova, rolling it up past the house.

Tucker hadn't moved.

Zeke thinking he could empty the clip before the man got a hand on the shotgun, saying, "Came to see how things were getting done."

"Who you think got shit done back when you were driving Marty around?" Tucker turned and walked into the barn.

Bending for Sticky's pistol, Zeke dropped it in a pocket, looking to see Sticky going back and closing the gate. Following Tucker into the barn, passing the double-barrel Winchester, he said, "Happened to the guy out in the corn?"

"You want, I can take you out there, show you where Sticky put him in the ground."

"He shoot him?" Zeke looking surprised.

"Finished the job you started. Cleaning up your mess, yeah. You want a look, make sure it got done right, we'll walk you out there."

"Take your word. Want to know about the drying and

169

curing." Asking Tucker about his crew, how many he had picking the weed.

"Could've done that with a phone call," Tucker said.

"Yeah, well, I'm a hands-on guy." Zeke looked up at the washing lines strung between the rafters. A couple of heaters, fans and a pair of generators at the back wall. Some of the crop already hanging, looked like a couple hundred plants so far. Plenty of room for more.

"Heard some guys use ovens," Zeke said, like he knew something.

"Yeah, you do that, and the shit dries too fast," Sticky said, coming in the barn. "Dark and dry, nice and easy. Too fast and you trap the sugars and chlorophyl. The weed ends up tasting like shit, and turns out weak as ditch weed."

"So you lower the temperature." Zeke stepping so he could keep them both in view.

"Uh uhn. Got to be at sixty-five, seventy, tops," Sticky said. "Humidity's got to be just either side of forty-five."

"Done this before, huh?" Zeke said, lightening up, looking from Sticky to Tucker. These guys maybe not as dumb as they looked.

"Growing pot's one thing Sticky knows," Tucker said.

"And the one making the bhang," Sticky threw in. And if Tucker wasn't standing right there, he would have started up about his days making Owsley blotter. Tell Zeke how he used to print the tiny images of Stanley Mouse and R. Crumb. Mr. Natural and the flying eyeball. Did it with the vegetable inks on the old Heidelberg after hours, the print shop out in New West, up until he got sacked. Tripping most of the time back then, Sticky buying the acid tartrate dissolved in methanol from some chemist he knew, using eyedroppers, hanging the printed sheets. Mixing up the vegetable inks, printing up the blotter and running the perf machine in the wee hours. Each square promising a microgram of cosmic tripping. Still had his stoner's scrapbook someplace. Sticky still getting the flashbacks from time to time.

"That got it covered, Zeke, answer all your concerns?" Tucker said.

Still looking around, Zeke's eyes went from the vacuum sealer to the tool chest and welding torch, stopping on the catapult, saying, "What the fuck's this?" Walking past Tucker's tool trolley, a bunch of wrenches, screwdrivers and a box of shotgun shells.

Tucker moved behind him, tempted to grab a wrench and bash him with it.

"This what I think?" Zeke walking around it.

"Like I know what you think," Tucker said, reaching a brace off the tool trolley, still looking like he might go at him.

"How far?" Zeke said.

"Far what?"

"Far's it shoot?" Zeke walking around it again, looking impressed, saying, "Like a giant slingshot, right?"

"Yeah, more like a catapult." Tucker pointed out the side door, across the marsh. "Gonna have her firing out to those trees."

Zeke looked out the side door, out to the grove of trees, saying, "Marty seen this?"

"Wanted to get it right before anybody saw it," Tucker said.

"Showed it to the girl," Sticky said.

Tucker raked him with a look, Zeke still walking a circle, checking it out, touching the sling, the trigger, figuring it out, saying, "I got to say, my man, this is something."

Tucker looked at him.

Zeke looking serious, saying, "So, you fire it, think you can hit the same spot every time?"

"What I'm going for, yeah."

"And you're thinking at night, right?"

"Yeah. Gets us around the patrols and choppers, nosey farmers on the other side."

Zeke going yeah, seeing how they could increase the business they had going with Murphy, the guy getting leery about doing business on the Canadian side since the tunnel bust, the DEA sniffing around. Zeke saying again, "So, Marty doesn't know, huh?"

"Not till I get it right. That or you go running your mouth."

"Won't hear it from me," Zeke said, both of them looking at Sticky.

"What the fuck am I gonna say?" Sticky said, "But you want something, I been thinking about making blotter acid. Like I used to, real quality stuff."

"Where are we, the sixties?" Zeke said. "Nobody wants that shit."

Tucker laughed, asking Zeke if he wanted a beer.

Zeke saying, "Why not."

Tucker telling Sticky to run to the house and fetch some. "And make sure they're cold." Then saying to Zeke, "Come out tonight, I'll fire something across, show you how it works."

"Sure like to see it." Zeke looking out at the fog hovering over the marsh, saying, "Sure could put it to work."

Looking out, Tucker said, "What the hell." Going to the row of pumpkins, thinking they could risk it. Calling after Sticky, telling him to bring that telescope, wanting to give Zeke a better look at that grove of trees on the U.S. side, telling him about the back road running right past it, nobody using it much anymore, a natural pickup point. Zeke forgetting the pistol he held down at his side, Sticky's in his pocket, the shotgun by the door.

Tucker readied the rig, blocking the soft tires and cranking a lever, setting the tension on the band, taking a pumpkin and setting it on what looked like a catcher's mitt, the three of them drinking beer. Sticky handing Zeke the telescope.

Tucker asked if they were ready.

"Let's see what you got," Zeke said.

Showtime.

Pulling the trigger, Tucker let it fly. Zeke putting the glass to his eye, watching the pumpkin's path, falling just short and east of the grove, but not bad, Tucker betting he'd get it right on the next try.

. . . DIRTY BACK ROAD

"Take all you can get," is what Murphy had told him. Didn't matter where it came from, Murphy not loyal to Marty Sayles or anybody else. Told Johnny he figured Zeke Chamas for a dumb fuck, betting he'd screw things up and get everybody busted. Guy always flashing that nickel-plated Colt, driving his muscle car, begging for attention. Told Johnny to call if he got his hands on any more. Johnny thinking if he timed this right, he'd be making that call. Had the idea to split down the coast with Frankie before these guys figured out who robbed them.

Driving his Scout nearly thirty miles down the 99, Johnny crossed the border at Blaine, showing his driver's license, saying he was just visiting a friend, finding his way along another nine miles of back roads, passing farms. Driving around till he found a tractor trail leading to the marsh, marking his own map so he could find his way back.

Making like a bird watcher, the binoculars hanging around his neck, he stepped out, going along the edge of the marsh, finding a spot behind a mossy rock, dry enough for him to squat down, the farmhouse on the Canadian side a couple hundred yards off. The fog hanging like a low ceiling.

Staying low, Johnny felt the cold and damp coming through his pants and shoes. He trained the field glasses on the farmhouse and turned the focus knob. Smoke plumed from the chimney, nothing happening for a quarter hour, then an old delivery van rolled down the townline and pulled to the gate, Sticky coming from the barn and swinging it open, letting the driver pull in and up to the barn. The hedge out front and the angle didn't give Johnny much more to see. From somewhere a hound bellowed, Johnny looking around. Geese flying in formation, heading south.

The morning chill was biting into him when the van rolled back down the drive and pulled away. Sticky closed the gate and went back into the house. Johnny's teeth started to chatter by the time the Nova rolled along Zero Avenue, heard it before he saw it, the grumbling of the headers rolling across the marsh.

Pulling into the drive, Zeke Chamas tapped the horn. Doing it twice more, longer each time. Sticky hurrying from the house, boots in his hand, stuffing his feet into them, pulling back the gate. Johnny grinning, watching these fools, thinking this could be easier than he thought.

Zeke rolled up the drive and Sticky closed the gate, the two of them stood there, looked like they were talking. Tucker coming from the barn, the three of them standing on the drive, Sticky tossing down his gun, Zeke picking it up and following Tucker into the barn, Sticky pulling the Nova up past the house. Johnny shaking from the damp and cold, rubbing his hands together, planning how to hit them, reminding himself it would be worth it.

Scrabbling closer for a better view, marsh water over the tops of his shoes, he wanted to get a look into the barn, guessing the delivery van had dropped part of the harvest. Had to happen before the first frost. And it sure was getting cold enough for it, Johnny trying to keep his teeth from rattling, his body shaking.

A cop car on patrol rolled along Zero, passing the farm and turning north at the intersection. A short time later, Sticky went back to the house, came out with what looked like a six-pack, going back to the barn.

When the side door of the barn opened, Tucker wheeled out his catapult, the yard partly obscured by the cedars at the front of the property. Johnny angled closer still, water up to his ankles, the muck grabbing at his soles, making a sucking sound when he stepped. Keeping low, not wanting the locals on the U.S. side to report anybody looking suspicious. Johnny not wanting to explain to state troopers he was just a bird-watcher with wet feet.

Staying low, Johnny watched them fire the catapult, followed the path with the glasses, catching the flash of orange, not sure what it was, looked like a head. Hearing it splash down with a hollow thud, maybe twenty, thirty yards off, he was thinking of Arnie.

Training the glasses, he lost sight of it, fighting the sick feeling. Turning the glasses back on the barn, he saw Zeke with the telescope up to his eye. Not sure if he'd been spotted, Johnny got as low as he could, not much cover where he was. Down on all fours with his pants and shirt getting soaked. Chancing a look, Johnny trained the field glasses and watched Tucker wheeling the catapult back inside. A few minutes later, the low grumble of Zeke's headers rolled across the marsh. Then the barn doors closed.

Knee-deep in the marsh, Johnny went searching around, dreading what he'd find. Shoes squelching as he stepped. Thigh-deep in the marsh water when he saw it: the fleshy carcass and spilled seeds and pulp like entrails. Nothing but a pumpkin.

Jesus Christ.

Turning from the thigh-deep water, he hung around long enough to catch a pickup with a cab roll down the townline and pull into the drive. Sticky coming and opening the gate again, the pickup pulling up to the barn. Definitely unloading the harvest.

Johnny turned the Scout around and drove out of there, knowing they'd be hanging all the weed in the next day or so.

Turning the heater and blower on high, he rolled down the side windows to keep the windshield from fogging up, shaking in the wet clothes, driving back to the Peace Arch, telling the guard at the crossing he got a bit excited about the snow geese and dabbling ducks, had nothing but wet feet to declare, telling the man he'd be coming back tomorrow, hoping for some trumpeter swans. The border guard suggesting thicker socks and a hot thermos. Johnny saying, "Yeah, for sure."

. . . THIRD BASS

Setting the two-fours on the bar top, Johnny watched Frankie pushing the sweep broom, pitching in on account of Arnie not showing up for work. She was hoping Johnny wouldn't fire him if that's all it was. She'd been too nervous to sit around her place. Waves of Nausea playing Falco's Nest tonight.

Reaching under the bar, he pulled up a stack of the handbills, setting them down, saying, "You see these?"

Frankie taking a look, leaning the broom against the bar. "Awesome." Picking up a handful:

> *Waves of Nausea*
> *this weekend at Falco's Nest*
> *Special guest, Wimpy*
> *Only two bucks to get in.*
> *Half buck cheaper than the Buddha.*

That got him a hug.

"Going up all over town," he said.

Frankie went behind the bar, kissing him.

Tearing open the top of a case, he put cans on ice, telling her about the kid, Jason, he hired from Strathcona Elementary. Soon as school let out, the kid papered the town, fast with the tape and glue-pot of flour and water, Jason pasting and tacking posters on hoardings, lamp posts, mail boxes, all over the Downtown Eastside, passing some out as handbills. Johnny paying him a couple bucks an hour.

She told him Wimpy was like a god on bass, his band without a gig tonight.

Johnny nodded, knowing him, the guy who brought crowd-surfing to town, like Vancouver's answer to Iggy Pop, a true wild man on a stage.

Frankie saying he'd come a long way from the days of the Bloated Cows. Still worried about Arnie, telling Johnny about the call from Shithead, her aunt jotting the message.

Bending for the dustpan, she swept up the trash and bagged it, went on talking about this west coast tour, asking if he'd heard about the Mab.

"You kidding? Right down in North Beach, kinda sleazy joint with strip clubs all around it. Filipino restaurant by day, hell of a place at night."

"Right." She said it was a dream to play a place like that. A chance to meet Jello and the Avengers, and the Flesh Eaters, and the Slashers. "It doesn't work out, maybe I can swing round a pole, peel down past my undies." Frankie thinking again about Marty saying she was five years past L.A., Zeke calling her "pasty ass." Still pissed off about it.

Johnny saying he'd like to see that, putting more cans on ice.

"Yeah?" Frankie smiling, saying it could happen. "Maybe give you a private show sometime."

"How about tonight." Johnny saying he'd bring the vodka. Then saying, "Things're looking up for you, that's for sure." Saying she deserved it.

Frankie dumped the pan in the bag, getting emotional and changing the subject saying, "So, what's up with robbing Marty?"

"Had eyes on the farm today," he said, telling her Zeke showed up, Tucker showing off his rig, told her about the pumpkin, thought they were firing it at him, not saying he thought it was a head.

"Like being attacked by Fred and Barney." Frankie laughing, trying to picture it. The idiots doing it in broad daylight.

Johnny telling her about the van and pickup pulling up, saying for sure they were harvesting, drying it in the barn. Had to be why Zeke was down there, playing the man in charge.

"So, you're hanging around, waiting for them to shoot the stuff over?"

"Can't see Marty letting them do it for real," he said.

Frankie saying one of Murphy's guys got nailed crossing last week, a couple pounds of bhang in his backpack. "Top of that, the cops busted that tunnel . . ." Frankie shrugged, could see Marty going for it.

"Doesn't matter, long as we get to it first."

"You thought more about how to get to it?"

He didn't have it all down yet. Coming at the barn from the cornfield out back seemed the best way. He'd need more than his Scout to haul it away. For sure, they had to do it at night. He'd be back across the marsh tomorrow, freezing his ass off, keeping his eyes on the place and picking his time.

"Think Arnie did something crazy, like went down there on his own, tried ripping them off?"

Johnny saying he didn't know.

"Just got a bad feeling, that's all," she said.

Johnny played it back, Arnie sweeping up when Monk drew him the map. Knowing Arnie overheard them talking, could have gone down on his own. And got caught. Not the first time he thought it, Johnny pushing it out of his mind for now, saying, "Sorry I started up about it. Let's just stick to tonight."

"Yeah." Frankie walked the trash out back, tossing it in the bin. Johnny watching her come back, getting an empty feeling, this girl with the chops, as good as Poison Ivy. Soon she'd be on the road, "No Fun City" becoming a hit, and the thing between them could end as fast as it started.

She picked a poster off the bar, smiling, then going around the bar, slipping her arms around the back of his neck, saying, "Do this for all the bands?"

"Yeah, I do, but still, there's perks for the ones I sleep with."

"Yeah, you sleep with the Wimp?" She tugged his shirt free, working at his buttons.

"Guy's good, no doubt, but not my type."

"Good to know," Frankie peeled off his shirt, starting on his belt buckle.

"Hey, whoa up . . . this a public place."

"Door's locked, right?"

"True." Hard to argue, he walked her backwards behind the bar, thinking they had about an hour before Stain and Monk would roll up. Asking if she wanted a drink.

Frankie hiking herself up on the bar, next to the cash register, pulling him close, saying, "Ask me after."

. . . HANDS SHAKING, KNEES WEAK

PULLING BEER tabs, Johnny set the cans on the bar. Hands reaching across for them, Johnny sticking the dollars in the till, it dinging every time he did. Falco's Nest was filling up fast. Punks lining at the door, Stain collecting two bucks a head.

Strapping on the Flying V, Frankie blew into the mic, Joey tapping his snare behind his drum kit, the stage lights on. A good crowd building in front of the stage, Frankie talking to people, feeling the heat of the lights. Looking through the glare, waiting for Wimpy to show. Her Philips recorder set up by the stage lights, the mic taped in place, a fresh c90 tape ready to record the gig.

Scanning around, Johnny guessed the room was hitting capacity: the fire marshal maxing Falco's at a hundred people. Some of those waiting to get in started filling up the alley around the Harley and Johnny's Scout, merging with the crowd out front.

The Buddha likely hit its capacity early, standing room only, the club stuffed like a sardine can. The K-Tels were on tonight, a band Frankie had followed since back in the days when they were the Shmorgs, hearing the company of the same name had their bloodsucking lawyers demanding the K-Tels change their name, not wanting any confusion between a Veg-O-Matic and a west coast punk band. Anybody who couldn't get into the Buddha was wandering down here, Falco's catching the overflow. "I Hate Music" heard from up the block. Both venues sure to raise some more noise complaints and heat on the night.

●

COULDN'T WAIT for Wimpy anymore, Frankie waved to the writer for the *Snot Rag*, then kicked off the set, plucking a lick from the old Bill Justis tune "Raunchy," feedback screeching through the speaker. Frankie giving them a medley, throwing in the run from "Rumble," punking up some Duane Eddy, then some "Miserlou" at the end. A hell of a solo.

Hands went in the air, some clapping, some waving beer cans, people starting to pogo. Joey Thunder adding a beat, the crowd getting into it. Frankie leaned to the mic, saying, "Hey, we're just getting wet here, right?"

A roar from the crowd. Johnny selling beer as fast as he could pull the tabs, suds all over the bar. Dollars stuffed the register.

When Wimpy stumbled through the door, Monk plowed a path for him through the crowd, practically having to lift the man's drunken ass onto the stage. The Wimp picking up Arnie's taped-up bass, yelling for the crowd to fuck off, the crowd giving it back, splashing him in beer. Wimpy loving the suds. Frankie rattling off another lick, the three of them getting into "Paint It Black." Putting some edge into it. Followed it with "Firing Squad," one of Wimpy's, Frankie helping him out on vocals.

The music thumped outside, Zeke Chamas pushing his way to Falco's door. People lined the sidewalk, drinking and toking, talking and laughing, passing joints and bottles. Stain caught Zeke cutting into the line and blocked his way, aware he was packing. Had to be here for the rent. Stain telling him, "No fucking way."

"Know who I am, right?" Zeke said, putting his hand in a pocket, reaching for the cover charge.

Stain caught his wrist, thumped a finger against his chest, told him they were full, told him to come back tomorrow. Zeke opening his mouth to speak, not getting the message. Grabbing him by the arm, Stain spun him around, scooped him by the nuts, closed his fist and put Zeke up on point. His free hand went under Zeke's jacket and pulled the shiny Colt. Sticking it in his own belt, Stain backed him through the line, calling out, "Coming through."

The line of people parted. Stain walked him out past the line before letting go. Zeke tottered, staying on his feet. The ache in his crotch was unbelievable. Had to force himself to breathe.

Checking up and down the block, Stain yanked the clip and shoved the pistol back in Zeke's pocket, saying to him, "Next time you come down here packing, you get gun-fucked." Didn't matter what the club prez said about not mixing it up with Marty Sayles's crew. Turning, he went back through the door. The crowd parting around Stain like it was swallowing him.

Inside, Waves of Nausea rocked the house, rolling into Menace's "Screwed Up," Wimpy singing. Frankie churning the power chords, Joey Thunder sweating under the lights, pounding the beat. Fans packed around the makeshift stage, pogoing and yelling and loving it, arms in the air. "Woke Up Screaming" was next, Frankie soloing her way into "Refugee," Wimpy spiraling off the stage, doing some crowd-surfing, getting passed from hand to hand.

Couldn't believe how fast he was going through cases of 50 and Ex, cans this time, no more bottles in here, Johnny sick of the broken glass, plus cans were lighter, and after that scene in the john . . .

Tossing the cardboard down by his feet, he stomped the cases flat. Getting Monk to watch the till, he made his way back to the storeroom for more beer, down to a couple dozen cases. Serving up room-temperature beer, no chance for them to get cold, but it didn't matter to the punks reaching across the bar. Two bucks a beer, Johnny was pulling off zip tabs as fast as he could. Man, he could have used Arnie tonight. Of course, Arnie should have been on the stage, Johnny wishing he was seeing him up there.

. . . FLESH MACHINE

Picking himself off the sidewalk, Zcke breathed through the ache in his crotch. Sure he was going to heave his guts. Betting his nuts would be blue for a week. The big dumb fuck had tossed his pistol down with a round left in the chamber. Zeke righted himself, some buck-toothed teen laughing at him, boot-black hair in spikes, ripped-up vest with no shirt and a bike chain swinging round his neck.

Catching the chain, Zeke gave it a twist, cutting his air and changing his attitude, asking if it was funny now, showing the nickel-plate to his buddies moving in. Letting go of the chain, Zeke went through the guy's pockets, finding a Baggie.

Zeke saying, "Dexies?"

The kid saying yeah, rubbing at his neck, Zeke guessing they were five mil, guessing they came from one of Marty's own street dealers. Clapping a few in his mouth, Zeke scattered the rest on the sidewalk, saying they were on the house.

Pressing his way through, shoving people aside, no way he was leaving without Marty's back rent. No way he was going back to driving Marty around in that fucking Toronado.

●

WIMPY WAS back on the stage, walking the bass lines for "Fever."

The crowd yelling for it. Jumping, beer splashing like rain. Frankie wailing about fever all night, her mouth to the mic.

Making his way to the room in back, Johnny stacked a few more cases, Ex and 50, relocking the door. Taking a break, Stain got Monk to cover at the door, nobody getting in until he got back from the can, his pockets stuffed with bills. Left pocket was for the club, right pocket was his. Stain keeping it fair.

Monk told the crowd at the door to fucking wait, leaned on the bar, keeping an eye on the till and the door at the same time, his big arms folded, waiting for Stain and Johnny to get back. Some drunk chick hanging on his sleeve, bleached hair crew-cut, hands working at his belt, clumsy and drunk, but getting his attention. Monk not known to miss an opportunity, he tugged her behind the bar, warning the people at the door, "Nobody fuckin' move."

Heads nodding.

Zeke Chamas shoved his way in and made his way past the bar. Eyes searching for Johnny Falco, spotting the other biker making out with some chick behind the bar, keeping an eye out for the one who roughed him up outside.

Guessing Johnny was getting beer from the back, pushing his way through.

•

BALANCING HIS beer can on the ceramic top, Stain stood at the urinal, a job that took both hands. Unzipping, he faced the graffitied wall.

Man, the smell. Stain thinking Johnny really needed to get himself a hazmat team in here. Enough was enough.

Zipping up, he took his can, hit the flusher and turned for the door, the band ripping up "Fever." Stain loving the way Frankie's band was doing it. Pulling the door, he stepped out and spotted Zeke Chamas moving through the crowd. The guy he just kicked out. Shoving bodies aside, Stain came up from behind him, done talking.

. . . FEVER

Locking the back room, Johnny carried the stacked cases, squeezing his way through, missed Stain dragging Zeke into the can. He made it to the bar and set the cases down, loving the way Frankie was ripping into the old Peggy Lee number. Monk was behind the bar, wrapped around some chick with a bleached crew cut.

Johnny started ripping into the cases of beer. Hands waving dollar bills across the bar, the mob thirsty. Johnny seeing the door was unmanned, punks jammed into the doorway, heeding Monk's warning, catching the show from there.

Johnny snapped off tabs, slapped an Ex in Monk's hand, the guy wearing fingerless gloves with a fat ring on every digit. Johnny asking what happened to Stain, Monk saying he went for a slash, be back any minute.

Trading cans for cash, Johnny kept looking to Frankie on the stage. The girl in her element. Gyrating, hair flying, singing into the mic.

Frankie was wet with sweat. Joey Thunder crashing out a solo, doing his Keith Moon madman chops, rolling them into "Lust for Life." Never played it before, something Wimpy wanted to try. An easy progression in A. Frankie hammering power chords and wailing the lyrics she knew, faking the rest.

The crowd packed in tight around the stage, wild and loving Waves of Nausea.

She ducked a flying can that bounced off a cymbal, another hitting the back wall of plastered handbills and spray paint. Wimpy unslung the bass and dove off the stage again. Kids trying to catch him, then dropping him, the man landing on the concrete, slow getting up, hands shoving him back onto the stage. Somebody passing him a fizzing beer.

●

Snatching a handful of shirt, Stain dragged Zeke backwards into the can, flinging him, Zeke slammed against the urinal. Head striking the wall, losing his footing, he ended sitting in the pisser, urinal cake soaking his ass. Felt like his arm was busted, pain shooting through him. The big man coming at him, grabbing him again.

"The fuck I just tell you?" Words and spit, Stain throwing him again. Smacking him into the sink, head smashing the grimy mirror. Zeke's legs gave out and down he went. The smell of piss. The floor wet under his hands.

Getting up, Zeke stumbled left, then right, tripping into the toilet, down on the floor again. Hand fumbling for the pistol.

Not worried about an empty gun, Stain came at him.

Pounding music drowning out Zeke's yelling. Waves of Nausea tearing into "Jailhouse Rock."

His back pressed against the black wall, Zeke pointed the pistol. Stain reached the clip from his pocket, holding it up. This badass forgetting he pulled it. Saying it was time for that pistol-fucking.

Couldn't hear the words, Zeke stuck the barrel into the big gut. The pistol bucked in his hand, the shot muffled.

Felt like he'd been punched, Stain reeling back, looking down like he didn't believe it, the dark wet spreading across his belly.

"One in the chamber, asshole," Zeke yelled over the music, aimed again and dry-fired. Flipping the pistol, he swung for the side of Stain's head.

Stain stayed on his feet. Catching and twisting the barrel away, he cuffed Zeke on the side of the head, doing it again, Zeke throwing his arms up, trying to ward off the blows, trying to back away. Stain tossed the pistol down, shoved Zeke against the sink, bent him backwards, hands clamping around his throat, squeezing, taking Zeke's air. The two of them head to head. Stain kept squeezing.

The dexies sparked like a charge, Zeke clutching at the hands, then letting go, grabbing at Stain's belly, like squishing bloody hamburger. Yelling, Stain let go, stumbling back, keeping to his feet.

Light and the rush of sound, some guy with a mohawk came in and froze in the doorway, then ran back out, wanting no part of what was going on.

Feet slipping on the bloody, wet floor, Zeke gasped for air, his throat felt crushed.

Stain went to one knee, middle of the floor, the fight going out of him, flopping to his side, his hands holding his gut, blood spilling on the floor.

Zeke was standing over him, sucking in air, felt like he was breathing through a straw. He threw a kick at Stain, the Frye boot with the two-inch heel. Stain down on his back, couldn't defend himself. Zeke kicking at his head, not much behind it, but smashing the nose, blood flowing from the mouth.

The door flew open again, and Monk rushed in, taking it in, yelling something Zeke couldn't understand. Zeke backing up, looking around, nowhere to go. Feeling for the blackjack in his pocket. Monk looked down at Stain, pulling his switchblade, letting Zeke see it coming.

. . . FUN WHILE IT LASTS

THE FIRST set had gone like a blur. Frankie's black hair matted to her head. Wasn't a drug that could do that — like a rock and roll orgasm. Finished up the set with Generation X's "Ready Steady Go." The crowd singing backup.

A guy with rose glasses was there from Perryscope, all smiles and thumbs-up. Nudged his way to the front of the stage, passing Frankie a card, making a phone with thumb and pinkie, telling her to call. That EP and tour down the coast was feeling real. Reaching out, she walked across the stage, slapping hands waving up from the crowd. Taking it all in. The lights bright and hot. Felt like heaven.

Never saw Monk coming from the can, blood all over his shirt, or Johnny rushing into the can, people milling around the door.

Frankie sat at the edge of the stage, Joey Thunder next to her, saying, "Played the hell out of that one." Wimpy going in search of more beer, cradling his arm from that last dive. Frankie and Joey talking about trying a few of their own tunes, starting the second set with "No Fun City."

Nothing unusual about the scream of sirens, especially

down here. But these grew louder, more than one, stopping right out front.

"Another fuckin' raid," Joey said. "Fuckin' noise complaint or the screws looking for a liquor license." Frankie and Joey getting up and looking to the front.

Paramedics rushed in with a gurney, pushing through the crowd, two uniforms assisting, ordering people back. More sirens. More cops coming in. Falco's Nest was being cleared out.

"What the fuck?" Frankie was up, yelling into the mic for the pigs to stop, get the fuck out, anything else she could think of.

One of the uniforms grabbed her off the stage, got her in a fireman's carry, lugging her out, another cop escorting Joey and Wimpy to the door, the place emptying. Frankie kicking and complaining, didn't want to leave her Flying V. The cop set her down outside, cuffed her hands behind her back, told her she was under arrest. Frankie yelling, "What the fuck for?" putting up a struggle, eyes searching for Johnny. The cop turned her face-first against the outside wall.

Wimpy and Joey Thunder ended up cuffed next to her along the wall. Then Johnny was pushed out, told to stand next to them, Johnny not wanting to leave the register unattended. The cop turned him and cuffed him, deaf to his protests.

Falco's Nest was cleared out, two uniforms standing by the door, another putting up perimeter tape, others keeping the crowd back, waving drivers along East Hastings who were slowing to have a look. Red and blue lights flashing.

People outside the Buddha were coming down for a

look, everybody crowding the sidewalk and street, wanting to know what was going on. Paramedics had come out with gurneys, two bodies under sheets, the ambulances driving away. Cops dispersing the crowd, not saying what was happening. A news van pulled up, a reporter and his camera man, microphones and cameras, the two of them getting as far as the yellow tape.

Cops were taking statements, asking for witnesses. The guy with the mohawk giving an account of what he saw in the can. The chick with the bleached hair stood near Frankie, crying, saying it was Stain, blood all over him, not sure who else.

Another patrol car screamed along Hastings, coming past Woodward's, then a paddy wagon. Those along the wall were put in back, the cops not saying more till they got to the station.

. . . SHEETS TO THE WIND

Spitzer was the detective asking questions at the station, sitting her down at his desk, treating her alright, had the uniform take off the cuffs, got her some water and box of tissues. When she stopped crying, Frankie thanked him, pointing to a sign on the washroom door across the hall: *Washroom for customers only*. Asking Spitzer, "That for real?"

Spitzer smiled. "Naw, one of the guys's got a sense of humor. Likely got it from some cafe or someplace."

"Stole it?" Frankie grinned, then asked if it was true, what she heard about the special elevator.

"The what?"

"One you cops used the night they raided the Buddha a couple months back, busting a bunch of punks, anybody else on the street out front. Cops throwing everybody in a paddy wagon."

"Heard about that, yeah," Spitzer said. "Punks punching and kicking the panels, spitting through the mesh, calling them pigs."

"Way I heard it, the cop driving slammed his brakes,

doing it over and over, everybody in back got tossed like a salad."

"Well, you give a cop attitude, it's what happens, right?" Spitzer said.

"When they got to Main, they got taken up in the special elevator, some of them beaten."

"Maybe depends who you hear it from." He looked at her. Getting around to his questions, Spitzer asked her what went down at Falco's. Frankie repeating what she already told the uniforms making the arrests, only calmer this time. Not much more she could add, being up on the stage the whole time it went down.

Making a couple of notes, Spitzer pushed the legal pad away and asked her about her music, admitted punk wasn't really his style, didn't understand it, saying he was more of a jazz man.

Frankie saying it was his age, Spitzer admitting it was probably true, still he wished her luck with it, heard from some of the kids they dragged in that her band was pretty hot.

"Heard that, really?"

"Yeah, bunch of times."

"Thanks."

Looking at her, he shrugged, pushed a business card across the desk, saying, "Anything else you want to tell me . . ."

She hesitated, then told him about Arnie being missing, explaining who he was, that he worked at Falco's.

"Something to do with this?"

She said she didn't think so. Spitzer wrote Arnie's name on the pad, Frankie saying she just had a bad feeling.

"Possible he's just gone off, you know, three sheets to the wind?"

She shrugged, then smiled and said they don't call it that anymore.

He tapped the pencil on the business card, saying if Arnie didn't turn up in a day or so to call him again. Frankie tucked the card in a pocket.

When they were done, he put her and Johnny in the rear seat of his unmarked Ford and drove them back to the club. A uniform stood outside, Falco's dark and locked up, Waves of Nausea posters in the window, yellow tape across the front.

All the evidence and photos had been taken, so Spitzer let them in, Frankie getting her guitar and amp. Johnny taking the cash from the register, slipping the Norton from under the rag and dropping it in a pocket when Spitzer wasn't looking.

... PRETTY VACANT

WATCHING HER from the sofa, Rita bit her tongue, knowing she'd just sound like a mom again. Rita just glad there weren't any obstruction or resisting charges laid.

"God, one minute I'm playing, then . . ." Frankie blowing her nose into the tissue.

Getting up, Rita went and put her arms around her.

"My buddy Stain . . ."

"I know." Rita hugged her.

"They closed Johnny down. Like it's his fault."

Rita holding her close, thinking Frankie could've ended up with a different kind of record, this girl who used to get straight A's.

The knock at the door had them both jumping. Rita going to it, expecting another cop with questions. Frankie getting up, too, smoothing her T-shirt, she didn't care about the eyeliner tears that had run like a river.

Rita opened it, Johnny Falco standing there. She let him in, closing the door behind him.

Frankie going to him, putting her arms around him, saying, "Sorry, I look like hell." Kissing him.

"You want coffee?" Rita said, going to the kitchen.

"Not if it's any trouble," he said.

Rita reached for the can of Maxwell House. Coffee you can count on. Then she reached into the freezer and took out a new bottle of Absolut.

Frankie held onto him, then went to the bathroom to fix her face. Rita asking him in the kitchen what happened. Johnny telling what he knew, pretty much the way Frankie had told it. Same way it had appeared on the evening news. Stain had been shot dead. Zeke Chamas, with a dozen stab wounds to the abdomen and chest, bled out before the paramedics rushed him to Van General. Cops calling it a drug deal gone sideways. No sign of Monk, the news calling him Caleb Haller. The cops putting out an APB. "Top it all, they shut me down."

"They say for how long?"

"Cops want to make it permanent, think it'll happen this time."

Frankie came back, the black gone from her face. "They can't do that."

"Yeah, they can. Got a stack of violations. Way the cop put it, they're stamping out a fad," Johnny said. "Cop said the Buddha's next."

Rita went about fixing the coffee, seeing this guy was just wrong for her niece. Frankie always latching on to the wrong guys, Rita knowing how it would end, same way it always did. Rita asking him, "How you take it again?"

"Black's good, thanks," Johnny said, sensing her aunt's mood.

Frankie got the mugs down, thinking it was time to

move on, get out of Rita's hair. She'd call Joey Thunder and talk about cutting the EP stateside. Get a hold of Swinson, the promoter down in Long Beach.

Another knock at the door, Frankie with her heart in her throat.

Rita went to the door, eye to the peephole. Another cop, this one with a badge on his belt and wearing a suit.

It was Detective Spitzer, saying he had a couple more questions, saying if Frankie was up for it, not looking surprised to see Johnny here. Rita asking if he wanted coffee.

Asking about Zeke Chamas, rumored to work for Marty Sayles. Asked about an incident at the club the other night, an altercation between Frankie and Sayles.

"Just a misunderstanding, nothing really," Frankie said.

"Okay, anything you can tell me about the Hellrazors?"

Frankie saying she knew it was a bike gang, knew Stain and Monk rode with them, but not much else.

Spitzer had a couple more questions, drinking the coffee Rita fixed him. With nothing to add to his notes, he asked if she'd heard from her friend, Arnie, the one she said was missing, one who worked for Johnny, looking at Johnny when he asked.

"No, not yet," she said, couldn't help glancing over at Johnny. Hadn't told him she had mentioned it to Spitzer.

"Could be on a bender, wouldn't be the first time. I don't know," Johnny said, "but, I got a question."

"Shoot."

"About reopening my club."

Making it sound sympathetic, Spitzer said it didn't look good. Scene of a murder and all. "Top of that, serving liquor to minors, doing it on an expired license. The place packed beyond capacity. A dozen noise complaints since you opened. You want me to go on?" Spitzer said, giving him that what-did-you-expect look.

"Don't need to," Johnny said. "I get the picture."

. . . LAST TORONADO

THE TWO of them sat in her Karmann Ghia, the heater on full, Frankie pushed in the lighter, waited for it to pop, dropping the last chunk of the black hash. Taking a toke, she offered it to Johnny, saying she was going down the coast. Not going to rob Marty Sayles.

Johnny didn't say anything, taking a toke.

"It's not going to fix anything."

Johnny shrugged, then they sat quiet, both looking across Hastings at his club, locked up with the crime scene tape across the front. *Closed till further notice* taped to the door.

A uniform stood by his patrol car, a tow truck driver hooking up Zeke's Nova out front, hauling it away to impound.

"These guys aren't playing," Frankie said, watching the cop get in his patrol car and drive off, "in case you haven't noticed."

Johnny nodded, thinking he'd do it alone, leave her out of it.

Then the Toronado pulled up, Marty Sayles and the

blonde looking in at them. Marty pulled up, backing to the curb in front of them.

"Oh, for fuck's sake." Frankie reached for the ignition, wanting to get out of there.

"Hold on." Johnny stopped her hand.

Stepping out in a camel-colored trench coat, Marty looked across at the yellow tape out front of Falco's Nest, smiling as he came around the back of his ride, sniffing like he had a cold.

"Keep her running," Johnny said, getting out and walking around the front, blocking Marty's path. Saying, "Get to drive yourself now, huh, Marty?"

"Unless you got my rent money, how about you shut the fuck up, get out of my way? Her I want to see, not you."

"But it's me you're going to talk to."

"That right, huh? Tell you what, clear your shit out, you're done here. How's that? Now we done talking?" Marty sniffed and went to pass him.

Hooking his sleeve, Johnny spun him around, starting to say, "Got nobody backing your —"

Getting enough hip into the punch, Marty let it fly, putting Johnny down. Shaking out his hand, saying, "You need, I can tell you some more."

Another patrol car drove along, the two uniforms seeing it was Falco on the ground, both of them smiling, seeing no crime in letting the guy in the coat hit him, the cops driving on. The sign on Falco's door meant they wouldn't get another chance to toss a wino through his door, tell him they were cleaning up the Eastside.

Frankie was out of her car, her bag in her hand, calling

the cops assholes, throwing them a finger. Tugging up her jacket, she stepped forward, setting her bag on the hood, saying to Marty, "You're really some kind of asshole, you know it, Marty?"

Sally, the blonde, got out of the Toronado, recognizing the bitch who knocked her out in Falco's can, the one to blame for the stitches in her head. Sally wanting some payback.

"Not the way I'd play it," Marty said to Frankie, sniffing, catching hold of Sally, keeping her back, the girl giving Frankie some mad-dog looks.

"Sorry about what happened to Zeke and the other guy, but you and me need to talk," Marty said.

"Yeah, you got an opening, huh?"

"Ought to hear me out."

"Yeah, the three of us sitting down, you, me and her, having a chat," Frankie said, glaring at Sally.

"Got things to work out," Marty said, watching Johnny getting up.

"You promised me," Sally whined, tugging to free her arm.

Marty shaking her arm, told her to chill.

"You want to talk," Frankie said, "how about you tell me what happened to Arnie?"

"Who's Arnie?"

"Think your guys caught him in the corn, helping himself to your weed."

"Yeah, right, heard about that, huh?" Marty sniffing, running a finger under his nose, seeing a smear of blood, saying, "You know how it works, somebody messes with me, I mess back."

"It was Zeke, right?"

"That guy . . . yeah, well, Zeke being Zeke, maybe he called me up, told me about the beating he laid on the guy. Arnie, think that was the name. Caught him ripping me off. My boys down there showing some initiative, taking care of business."

"What's that mean?"

"Got to spell it out?"

"Where is he, Marty?" Frankie putting her hands in her pockets.

"Why don't you go talk to them?" Marty not saying anymore about it.

Johnny was up on his feet, Frankie holding up a hand, meaning for him to back off.

"You want your job, maybe we work things. Just looking for a yes or no."

Sally yelling, "No!"

Marty shaking her, saying to Frankie, "Same as before. Only this time, nobody's in between."

"You promised me." Sally pouted. Too high for reason, she flapped her arm free, rushing at Frankie, putting up her hands, the stick-on fingernails like claws.

Hand coming from a pocket, Frankie had the pink gun out and maced her, a stream like a dog pissing.

Sally shrieked, hands going to her eyes, staggering off the sidewalk, stumbling into the street. A Plymouth honked and swerved. Yelling her eyes were on fire, Sally lurched left, then right, out to the dividing line, cars honking from both directions. A homeless man went out to her, calling her sister, leading her to the opposite sidewalk, sitting her at the curb out front of Falco's.

"Still some left," Frankie said, pointing the pink gun at Marty.

Marty looked at her, then turned back to the Toronado.

"Want to know what you did to Arnie," Frankie yelled.

"For that, you need a shovel."

"What did you do, Marty?"

"Same as I always do. Took care of fucking business." Opening the door, he swung into the seat, looking across at Sally on the curb, slamming the door, yelling, "Fuck." Then pulled into the lane and screeched off.

Frankie watched the Toronado pull away, looked at Johnny holding and moving his jaw. She dropped the pink gun in her pocket. The two of them looking across the street at Sally, sitting at the curb, the fight out of her, the homeless guy sitting next to her and consoling her.

"You're something, you know it," Johnny said.

"You think that was something . . ." Frankie reached her bag off the hood, the mic practically hanging out. She pulled up the Philips recorder, the one she'd used at dozens of gigs, pressing the button, turning it off, saying, "Hope I got enough." Hitting rewind, playing it back, the voices clear enough.

"The hell you want to do with that?"

"Drop it off." She pulled out the card that Spitzer gave her, showed it to him.

"Could blowback, they start looking into Marty's business."

"Yeah, not going to hang around to find out. Say you and me head down the coast?"

"Yeah?"

"Yeah," Frankie said, looking over at the blonde. "Think they got all that pot in the barn yet?"

"I thought you said . . ."

Taking her bag, she went to get back in, looking across at the blonde, saying, "Maybe I changed my mind."

. . . ZERO AVENUE

WALKING A couple of miles of Zero Avenue, Johnny hoped they timed it right. They had stopped at the cop station on Main, Frankie dropping off the cassette, left it for Detective Spitzer, told the sarge at the desk it was tied in with an investigation. The two of them hoping it was as good as a confession, Marty Sayles admitting he had a part in having Arnie killed.

Stopping off at her aunt's place, Frankie packed a bag, took her guitar and amp, left a note on the counter. The two of them driving to his place, leaving the Karmann Ghia in his parking spot, Johnny grabbing a few things, the two of them driving off in the Scout.

Dropping Johnny off a few miles east of the Peace Arch, the idea was he'd walk as Frankie drove across the border, making her way along the back roads on the U.S. side, following the map Johnny drew. Her Flying V and amp on the back seat between their bags.

•

A ROW of suburban houses stood along Zero Avenue, all looking the same, built back at a time when folks had their milk delivered, the small door at the side, the delivery man leaving glass pints and quarts. The suburb part gave way to older farmhouses, trees and fields, cows lowing. Zero Avenue running straight as a ruler. Washington State across the ditch, nothing but the odd marker and brambles separating two countries. Johnny thinking of the tunnel the cops busted, had to be right along here. Some farmer reporting suspicious behavior to the Mounties.

The sun looked more like the moon, showing pale and small through the fog, Johnny feeling the morning damp, passing the field where Frankie stopped to pee, smiling about it now. About a mile to go. Johnny thinking about that night, showing up at the barn, Arnie's bass in his hand, sitting in. Wishing he had taken Arnie along when he robbed the pot field, sure Arnie had gone back on his own. Likely got caught and then killed.

Guilt hung heavy. Johnny wanting to set things right, telling himself he was doing this for Arnie. For Stain, too, the big man dying in the can like that, Zeke Chamas found halfway out the window, his body draped, looked like he died trying to climb out into the alley, blood dripping down the tiles, half-filling the sink, ruined his fucking boots.

Monk was likely on the run now. A Canada-wide warrant for his arrest. Whatever was left of the Hellrazors helping him to disappear. Johnny hoping he made it.

The rusty gate was just ahead, the fog getting thicker, the old farmhouse coming into view past the cedar hedge, Johnny smelling wood smoke, seeing it rise from the chimney. Taking the .22 Norton from his jacket, he checked the rounds, dropped it back in the pocket. Adding a little surprise, he hoped it was enough. Looking across the marsh where he'd hid two days back, the fog shrouding it now, hoping she'd be waiting for him.

Turning up the drive, he swung a leg over the gate, the wood creaking, his eyes on the front window. The barn doors hanging open. Murphy's white van sat out front, the kind delivery guys drove.

Shit.

Murphy was standing by the barn door talking to Tucker, first to see Johnny coming.

Tucker looked and saw him, too, his twelve gauge leaning by the door. Tucker grinning.

... SNITCHED

DETECTIVE SPITZER showed up at Marty Sayles's door with two uniforms, the squad car in the driveway. Marty opened the door, looking surprised in his robe and slippers, sniffling, white powder around his nose. A red-haired woman behind him, Marty telling her to go put on some clothes and fix some coffee.

Showing his shield, saying who he was, Spitzer told Marty he wouldn't have time for that, wanted Marty to come down for questioning, told him they had coffee down at the station.

"Make it sound like I should call my lawyer."

"That part's up to you." Spitzer told him he had two minutes to get changed. The two uniforms looking serious, like Marty might jump.

"I got rights, pal," Marty said, "Think it's my first time, getting razzed by cops?"

Pointing at his nose, Spitzer said, "Might want to get a tissue."

Down at Main, Marty sat in the metal chair, hands on the table, sniffling and not talking.

Spitzer sat across from him, waiting, saying, "You hear about Zeke Chamas?"

"Not till my lawyer shows." Marty said.

"The guy working for you like for about a year, playing chauffeur when your license got lifted?"

Marty folded his arms, waiting, Marty not saying anything.

"How about Frankie del Rey, that one ring a bell?"

Marty sniffed.

Spitzer had taken the cassette Frankie dropped off to the Crown attorney, who took it to a judge. The tape had PUMPS gig handwritten on the label, scratched out in ink. Marty's voice clear enough. Spitzer waiting to hear, expecting he'd be detaining Marty Sayles past the twenty-four hours, the man not making bail.

When Marty's lawyer showed, he put on the two-hundred-buck-an-hour bluster, telling Marty to say nothing, promising he'd have him out in no time, these cops with nothing.

Spitzer smiled at Marty and his suit, this part of the job made it all worthwhile. On top of the tape Frankie del Rey dropped off, he had a sworn statement.

Almost like he read Spitzer's thoughts, Marty said, "That lyin' bitch Frankie accuse me of something?" Marty calling him pig.

Now Spitzer said nothing. Giving him and the suit a smile. The statement had come from Sally Cook. Marty's blonde had come filing a complaint against Frankie del Rey, claimed she'd been maced. With his pad and pencil, Spitzer asked Sally Cook some questions. Turned out she was more pissed at Marty than she was at Frankie, Marty leaving her at the curb on Hastings and just driving away. Sally spilled what she knew about his operation, how she overheard Zeke Chamas and Marty talking about this guy Arnie getting capped in a cornfield.

Marty was calling Spitzer a cocksucker when the uniform came in and whispered in Spitzer's ear. Spitzer grinned at Marty, and if it wasn't for his suit sitting next to him, he would have asked the uniform to take Marty around back to the special elevator, the one Frankie had talked about, where guys like Marty got off looking worse than when they got on.

His lawyer looked worried now, trying to settle his client, keeping him in his chair, Marty barking that he had rights.

Spitzer saying yeah, but wondering if he really understood them.

... CROSSFIRE

"WANT TO know what happened to Arnie," Johnny said, walking up the drive.

Murphy moved to the back of his van, closing the doors, leaving the mailbag by Tucker's feet.

"You got to be high coming here," Tucker said, looking down the driveway. No car out there, nobody else around, this guy dumb enough to come alone, and on foot.

Sticky stepped from the side door of the house, walking up behind Johnny, the pistol in his belt. Murphy going to the driver's door, didn't like being in the middle of something shaping into a shootout with him in the crossfire. Johnny guessing the van was loaded with the pot from the harvest, all cured and ready to go. Johnny coming a day late.

"Ask you again, about Arnie Binz," Johnny said.

Tucker shook his head, took a step to his left. The shotgun leaning by the barn door.

Sticky flanked Johnny, his Colt tucked in his belt. Twenty feet away before he stopped. This guy with nowhere to go.

Murphy saying he was out of there, opening his door, giving a sympathetic look to Johnny, saying, "Can let myself out." Closing the door, he started the van and rolled down the drive, not looking at Johnny again.

"Arnie, huh, guy who works for you?" Tucker said.

Johnny turned enough to keep both men in sight. Taking Sticky for more of a talker than a shooter, Johnny would go for Tucker first if he had to, the big man taking another step, the shotgun nearly in reach.

"I'll tell you, but understand," Tucker said, "it's not something that leaves this place."

"So tell me." Johnny put his hands in his pockets, making it casual.

"Was Sticky took care of Arnie." Hand reaching the shotgun barrel, lifting it. "Gonna put you in the same hole. Two of you together."

Sticky licked his lips, his mouth gone dry, taking a stance, trying to put on a show, his palms wet.

Johnny saying to Sticky, "You still got time . . ."

"Not me running out of it."

Johnny shrugged, looking back to Tucker.

Tucker held the barrel low, finger on the front trigger, saying, "That all you want, huh, ask about this guy Arnie?"

"Was hoping to grab some more weed while I was here, but looks like I missed my chance."

"Was you, huh, yeah, figured that," Tucker said.

"Had my eyes on the place the past couple days," Johnny said, nodding out toward the marsh, still all in fog. "Saw you were drying. Guess you rushed it. That or I misjudged it a bit."

"Could've gone longer, true, but Marty's been getting edgy, especially since that fuck Zeke got himself killed. Shit like that draws attention," Tucker said, watching Murphy hurrying to open the gate and driving off.

"Yeah well, guess I'll take the cash then." Johnny guessing it was in the mail bag by Tucker's feet.

Tucker laughed, saying, "Waste this fuck, Sticky."

"Ought to know the cops been called," Johnny said.

"Yeah, got a phone in your shoe?" Tucker said. "Like on *Get Smart*?"

"Was Frankie made the call," Johnny glancing across the marsh, saying, "Gas station in Blaine. Over there waiting for me now."

"That right?" Tucker looking out at the fog, saying maybe he'd go see her sometime.

"Girl caught Marty on tape this morning, your boss all coked up, admitting about Arnie getting killed, giving his say-so and naming you two bozos as doing it."

"Bullshit."

"Dropped the tape off on the way over here, detective she got chummy with last night, took her statement after your boy Zeke got himself killed. Trouble is, the bullshit got my club shut down, and being that he worked for Marty, way I see it, you fellas owe me."

Tucker saying, "You pull, Sticky, I back you up."

"Told you, it's Lenny Lowe," Sticky said.

The sound of a car engine racing up the gravel road, Johnny smiling.

Tucker jerked up the double-barrel, Johnny firing the Norton through his pocket, the bullet pinging into the door above Tucker's head. Johnny diving as Tucker got off a wild round, Johnny feeling the sting graze his shoulder.

Sticky drew his pistol on Johnny, an easy shot, looking at Tucker, saying, "How the fuck you miss with a shotgun?"

"Let me try again." Tucker fired the second barrel, hit Sticky full in the chest, knocking him back, putting him flat on the ground.

Sticky's pistol falling from his fingers.

Snatching the mailbag, Tucker ran into the barn, fumbling the box of shells off the tool trolley.

The sirens getting louder.

Sticky moved a leg, gagging on his own blood. Johnny scrambled up and ran up past the open doors and threw himself against the barn boards. The next blast of the twelve gauge had tore up chunks of board, leaving fragments hanging.

Dropping to all fours, Johnny heard distant sirens coming fast. Ignoring the burn in his shoulder.

The first VPD car pulled up to the gate, both doors swinging open. Cops yelling, drawing their weapons, aiming across their doors at the far side of the barn. Another cop car swerving in behind the first. Spitzer getting out of the passenger side, pretty sure he spotted Johnny.

Ducking low, Johnny ran along the east side of the barn, chancing a look through the opposite door. Tucker was on the far side, working the catapult's ratchet, loading the mail bag onto the sling, grabbing the shotgun, firing a volley at Johnny, then another one at the cops. Hitting the rig's trigger, he let it fly. Then, dropping the shotgun, he ran around back of the barn. The cops behind the squad car returning fire.

Johnny ran around the other side, in time to see Tucker plunge into the corn.

The cops were moving past the farmhouse, two with sidearms drawn, one with a pump shotgun, all watching the mailbag fly out over the cedars, entering U.S. airspace.

Spitzer stooped, checking Sticky's vitals, the guy splayed out like he was making snow angels. Two of the cops circled the barn, the one with the riot gun ran through the open doors. A fourth cop jerked open the farmhouse's screen door and went about securing the house.

More sirens on the way.

Johnny ran into the corn, hearing Tucker running ahead of him, crashing between the stalks. Running past where the pot had been, all the plants gone now. Tucker cutting east across the fallow field. Catching his breath, Johnny ducked low, going right, hearing the cops coming behind him. Sirens everywhere.

Staying down as two of the cops rushed past him between the rows, Johnny crept forward, seeing Tucker running for the townline road, the cops giving chase, yelling for Tucker to stop. Spitzer came searching for Johnny, coming along the rows. Johnny's hand finding the root Arnie had chopped, he threw it across the rows. Spitzer going in the direction of the sound, Johnny stepping over some soft ground, no time to think about it. Moving low along the edge of the fallow field, going in the opposite direction, working his way west along field. When he'd gone a couple hundred yards, he made his way along a fence line, cut down to Zero Avenue, getting in the ditch. Another cruiser sped past, its howler and lights going, two cops inside, neither seeing him.

Murphy's van was farther up the road, stopped on the shoulder, a pair of cruisers with flashing lights blocking the road. Johnny walked across, Spitzer somewhere behind him, shouting for him to stop. He half-turned and looked at him, Spitzer pointing his pistol at him.

Looking at him a moment, Johnny hopped in the opposite ditch, pressing his way through the brambles, getting clawed as he went through, the marshy water cold on his feet, the fog shrouding him, lending him cover. Half expecting a bullet, he was on the U.S. side before he turned and waved goodbye, Spitzer somewhere behind him. His shoes squelched as he stepped. He sank to one knee, tugging the leg free. He couldn't see the grove through the fog, but he kept moving to where he thought it was, where Frankie waited. He took the Norton and flung it as far as he could, hearing it splash down. Looking back again, there was no sign of Spitzer or the sound of anybody coming behind him.

. . . THE DROPPING DOLLAR

DRIVING THE back road, both hands fighting the wheel, Frankie bounced off the seat, bumping her head on the headliner. Rolled through another pothole, trying to get the hang of the Scout's clutch, the three-speed manual a little touchy, a damned uncomfortable ride on account of the heavy-duty suspension. Frankie trying to work around potholes created by the last rains. The fat tires slinging muck and gravel, pelting the undercarriage.

Johnny had shown her how to lock the hubs back at Rita's place, just in case she found rough spots in the road, but she didn't want to stop and step out. Hoping the bouncing wouldn't cause Johnny's player to eat the tape, the recording she made of Private School: "Money, Guns and Power," the B side filled with tunes off the compilation LP, one with Tim Ray, Wasted Lives, Exxotone and Active Dog, the music thumping.

Fog hung low to the ground, no way to see the grove of trees, just the old farm on this side that Johnny had marked on the map. Driving along, she switched the headlights off, looking, leaning across the steering wheel.

Startled by a jackrabbit darting across the dirt track in front of her.

Jesus.

Hoping she had got it right, nothing marked back where she turned off D Street, taking a back road, then another, then one that seemed more of a dirt track than a road, the wipers sloshing across the windshield. She heard the distant howl of sirens between songs. Guessing it was Spitzer. She'd fed the coins into the pay phone and made the call to the detective back at the gas station in Blaine, a place called the Pit Stop: two pumps under an island, a Coke machine, a power pole and a couple of trash cans. Told Spitzer where to find the farmhouse where Marty Sayles stashed his weed. Told him his crew was curing it now, then she hung up. The gas station attendant pointing her in the general direction of D Street.

She switched off the player now, easing the front tires through yet another pothole. Guessing she had to be close to the grove, watching out the windshield, wiper blades swishing across.

Something flew into the road, looked like wings flapping, landed with a thump in front of her. Frankie yelped, slamming the brakes as the wheel rolled over it, nearly put herself through the windshield, her chest banging the steering wheel. First thought, she hit a goose or another jackrabbit.

Getting out, she looked under the Scout, thinking the poor thing was dead, looking mangled. Gray and lifeless. It took a moment to register that it was canvas, not fur or feathers, the strap of the mail bag, a reflector stripe and zipper across the top. Taking a breath, she prodded it with a foot. Reaching down, she picked it up, unzipping the bag.

Holy shit.

Fingers going through the stacks of cash, the bag stuffed with bundled twenties. Looking around, laughing, thinking she just hit the jackpot. Looking into the fog, waiting for another bag to drop. Frankie guessing by the distant sirens Tucker didn't want to get caught with incriminating cash so he fired it over, overshooting the grove, hoping to come out later and find it.

Still laughing, she tossed the bag behind the seat and made a three-point turn, got the Scout facing west, looking to where Johnny would be coming from. She had told him he was crazy to go alone but understood why he needed to do it, promising she'd stay in the Scout, hoping she'd get a chance to tell him again.

She let the engine idle long enough to defog the windshield, then turned it off, leaving her window rolled down. Frankie putting her mind on heading down the coast with this guy she was getting to know, meeting up with D.O.A. on their tour, Frankie with no bass player. Joey Thunder promising to meet her in Seattle, said they could all stay with some chick he knew from when he went to art school.

She counted the bundles, twenty-five of them. Fanning the bills, fifty bills per bundle, she counted them twice, doing the math. Hearing him before she saw him, splashing across the marsh. Johnny walking out of the fog, his pants and shirt clinging to his skin, his hair matted.

"Jesus, thought I got turned around," he said, smiling. His whole body shaking.

She got out and ran to him, threw her arms around him. Didn't matter she was getting soaked, too. Kissing him, she walked him back to the Scout, seeing the holes in his jacket, asking if he was alright. Johnny saying he could use something hot. "Coffee, maybe a stack of pancakes."

"Yeah, think I saw a place," she said, getting behind the wheel, sure there was a coffee machine back at the service station. Putting the blower on full, she had him roll the passenger window down to keep the glass from fogging up again, Johnny shivering on the passenger seat, Frankie driving and watching for potholes, saying, "So, you done with it?"

"Yeah."

She wanted to know what happened, wanted to know about Arnie. The station came into view, she looked at him, saying, "First, got a little something, kind of a surprise."

"Had enough of bad ones." He put his hands in front of the fan, couldn't stop the shaking.

"Think you'll like this one." Reaching behind the seat, she pulled up the mail bag and set it in his lap.

ACKNOWLEDGMENTS

THANK YOU to everyone who had a hand in *Zero Avenue*: my publisher Jack David, Rachel Ironstone for her edits, and everyone at ECW Press who worked on the book. Also to my amazing editor, Emily Schultz; copy editor, Peter Norman; and designer David Gee for nailing another great cover. And finally, to my son Xander for giving this book its first read, helping with Frankie's song lyrics and sharing his knowledge of the indie music scene.

At ECW Press, we want you to enjoy this book in whatever format
you like, whenever you like. Leave your print book at home and take
the eBook to go! Purchase the print edition and receive the eBook free.
Just send an email to ebook@ecwpress.com and include:
  • the book title
  • the name of the store where you purchased it
  • your receipt number
  • your preference of file type: PDF or ePub?

A real person will respond to your email with your eBook attached.
Thanks for supporting an independently owned Canadian publisher
with your purchase!